Lesbian Plus
Ashley Bradley

Octavia scoffed into the phone.

"*Florida?* Why don't you just set me on fire and burn me alive instead?"

She'd received a call from her publisher informing Octavia a library in Gator Gunk, Florida had expressed interest in having Octavia come down and do a reading of her latest novel. Apparently her latest book, Horny 4 The Holocaust: Skinty Peen Edition was the one of the most requested e-novels at the Gator Gunk Gas Station Grill and Book Room/Rest Stop.

Octavia had been shocked to hear this news. She had no idea there were libraries in Florida; that even people from there could read. That was the initial shock. *"What the fuck is a Book Room?"* She thought her publisher was joking, doing a troll, and she got unreasonably angry. She didn't like people playing on her phone. She considered going back to her cornrows and Timbs days and pulling up, but then as the publisher kept on, Octavia realized possibly she was being completely serious.

"Apparently they're wild for your titles," the publisher went on. "They're apparently also huge stans of your effort 9/11: George Bush Did It, and All Five of My Holes".

Octavia thought how unprofessional it sounded for her publisher to be talking about "stans". Though she had found her publisher from a business card falling out of her Quiznos chinchilla wrap, some time back. The business card just fell out whilst Octavia was adjusting the wrap, trying to get it to look less slimy and noxious and actually like something her stomach would begrudgingly accept without roiling over upon itself with a tsunami and promptly rejecting it via her esophagus or anus in a violent hot, liquidy stream of *No, ma'am.* Octavia had looked at the card and thought: What fortune! Then she looked up and saw some mildew-hued woman humidly waving at her from behind the Quiznos toaster machine. The woman who was presently her publisher, and trying to send her to Florida to be eaten alive by an alligator, or one of those retarded criminals from the movie *Bully*. Octavia reconsidered the origins of how she came to be acquainted with her publisher and decided everything was going as expected, actually.

Octavia had grown a minor following self-publishing in the Erotic Trauma category. It was niche but not *niche niche*. There were tons, actually, of erotic Holocaust novels on the market. Erotic Pilgrims meeting the Indians and then killing them with smallpox blankets ebooks and novellas. Tons of erotic slave shit. Erotic Hashtag Free Britney. Erotic The Bombing of Hiroshima. Erotic I Thought Jurassic Park Was Real. All that kind of thing. Octavia wasn't surprised to hear her 9/11 erotica was popular. Erotic 9/11 actually was *niche niche*. Not a lot of titles there, surprisingly. Octavia had been warned it was still "too soon", but it was never too soon to bust a nut, she felt, and that title turned out to be her most popular next to, obviously, her erotic Holocaust, that she'd only published a few months prior. It was the first book she'd published under an actual publishing house (Miss Mildew). It was a small little imprint (The publisher's main job was toasting shit at Quiznos, still). It wasn't one of the big ones where they send you on tour and you get to brag at colleges about how you never even completed your degree but you still became a success and are super rich anyway. The publishing house was useless, actually. The only thing they offered was a professional-seeming outfit for shitty little Florida libraries to call to request an appearance to have something to do at their book place which generally just serves as a makeshift homeless encampment.

Octavia wrote all her books at the library so she was familiar with how useless and cringe they were. No one went there or did anything there who didn't have to be there because they had nowhere else to go during the day. So being asked to come and do a reading at one wasn't some accomplishment. But still she felt kind of tingly with anticipation. She'd never been asked to read anywhere before. Sure, it was at a library and not somewhere respectable like by the free mini-sausage samples at Costco, or in an entirely empty Barnes and Noble. No, nowhere respectable like that, but still. Someone, maybe even multiple people--even if they were all completely without purpose and likely deranged--had read her books and desired to have her come out and do a read-aloud.

Octavia briefly wondered if this was actually just a trick to recruit her into human trafficking. The more she thought about it. She considered if she even minded. Her day job was driving a school bus, and in between school bus driving hours she did food delivery for the apps and also meals-on-wheels. She'd been banned from half the apps already because she refused to get out of her bus even once when she made the deliveries, only ever tossing the orders from her bus window or bus door, and not really caring if the items typically splattered out onto the road or sidewalk, and then she'd been reported multiple times at the meals-on-wheels gig for delivering half-eaten meal trays to the helpless and needy. She had thought that most of the people signed up for that program were invalids who were too frail and sickly to be able to pick up a phone to call and complain about their missing mashed potatoes, but apparently a lot of them have like disabled people phones and shit and even the old ones have figured out texting, it was terrible.

"They'll pay to have you out," the publisher went on. "There's a little motel connected to the back of the library - they'll give you a free room. And complimentary Quiznos."

"Nothing complimentary about Quiznos," Octavia said, considering.

After a while she asked, "What's the pay?"

"A per diem, and they'll pay for a bus ticket. The Grey Butt Bus. So you'll be on it awhile, and there'll be cannibals, but it'll be free!" the publisher responded in good cheer.

Octavia thought about it.

"When is it?" she sighed. Was she really thinking about doing this? She was in her forties now. She forgot all the time. She still felt like she was twelve and crushin' on that new Puerto Rican kid that'd come to their school during the second half of the year. All the girls had a crush on him. He was lightskin with a caesar cut. He had a diamond earring. His name was Doug, but despite that, still managed to be the most popular boy with all the girlies. He'd pushed out Devon Watkins, the previous Number 1 Child Hottie. Devon had a bum leg but his face card never declined, even though his leg card did every time. Devon would hop around and the girls would be hopping along right after him. That is, until Doug Hernandez hit the scene. Then it was: Devon, *who?* He still had devotees, but his fan club had thinned considerably.

Octavia had never boarded the Devon train. He'd bullied her for a few weeks once back in elementary school. Made fun of her for being fat and having a moustache. Called her Charlie Fats, which didn't make any sense and wasn't a thing, but the kids laughed anyway and Octavia was pregnant not just with tasty cakes, but also permanently-scarring, unendurable embarrassment. She tried to shave off her moustache and got a whoopin' from her grandmother for ruining her "good razor". Fast forward to middle school and Devon had lost interest in bullying Octavia. She still was fat and had a moustache, he'd just slightly matured. He no longer tried to be the funny guy, probably because he "got hot" (for a middle schooler), so didn't need to put on a whole production, plus some of the braver kids he'd tried to bully roasted him for his leg so he was wise enough to eventually figure out kids would notice his dead leg less if he didn't give them a reason to have to.

The other reason Octavia never went for Devon was because he actually looked like a boy. He was boy entirely. Not vaguely feminine like a lot of the boys during that time. Octavia didn't know it yet back then, but she was Team Lesbo. In retrospect, Octavia could see Doug looked like a pretty little girl. Even with his short hair and being named Doug and that strange, deep, manly voice he had. Even with the fledgling moustache that rivaled Octavia's - he looked like a pretty little girl. Prettier than all the girls in their class combined. And there was a really TV-pretty girl back then named Olivia who did the pageant scene and always won first place even though her only talent was biting. Doug was prettier even than Olivia. That Year of Doug was probably the happiest Octavia had ever been. And sure she had given birth or whatever; and her son, he was cool, but nothing compared to the second semester of seventh grade and the first semester of eighth grade when she was totally in love with the boy who looked like a gentle, mustachioed little girl.

The second half of eighth grade, Octavia got her period, and heavy, low breasts that made her look like someone's diabetic great aunt. She also began taking karate and started crushing on her karate teacher who was a fifty year old homosexual Korean man with a long fuzzy ponytail and that became her sexuality for like two years, and ushered in her darkest days.

Octavia snapped back to the present, forty-six, and feeling vaguely like she wanted to die. But not really *die be dead die*. Maybe it was that she wanted a change, to have a different life, be doing different shit, but she was too lazy to make anything happen. Even the smallest most menial task felt insurmountable and impossible. She tried to remind herself that she had done things, made moves. She had a kid. That takes some semblance of effort. It's a total upheaval to have a kid. She took care of him. He was still alive, after eight years, and that takes some doing. She had a job. Driving a bus wasn't like, mad easy. She had to learn how to do it. She got her certificates and then she got the job and every day, five days a week, she drove a giant ridiculous dangerous ass machine out on the roads, carrying loads of precious (in theory) cargo safely to and fro. Only two kids had died so far on her watch, and one was from an asthma attack and another was because he'd been beaten to death at the back of the bus and Octavia couldn't hear anything to stop it because the bus motor was like really loud, so it'd been ruled not her fault and she was only suspended for like a day, with pay.

She was a writer. It took some effort to write shit. Especially 9/11 erotica with a prominent DP threesome starring George Bush and Osama Bin Laddy. That takes something of a person to think of and write down and make work. She wasn't just swimming aimlessly around the void, suspended without purpose or direction.

Octavia wondered if she was reaching, and none of that was really anything. Tons of people had kids and rode buses and wrote books. But not *everyone*. Maybe it meant something that she'd done things not everyone had done or could do.

Still, she felt every one of her forty-six years and she was tired. She was over it, but that feeling of exhaustion was overpowered by the gnawing, anxious feeling she had that she'd not done a thing. It was only the beginning, and she needed to get up-

"They want you next week," the publisher was saying.

"Alright," Octavia said without thinking. *"Aight,"* she corrected. She forgot usually she pretended to be a ghetto baby mama on the phone with the publisher so she would think Octavia was too simple to conduct business meetings over Zoom.

Am I allowed a guest? Octavia almost said, then fixed it to, "Can I bring some of my homegirls?"

The publisher laughed. "Sure, bring whomever you'd like. The more the merrier! They'll have to pay their own way, of cour-"

"See if you can get them comped Grey Butt Bus tickets. I know my homegirl Philly aint got no coin. She just put something down on her man's child support. Also I gotta bring my son cuz his daddy not answerin' the phone."

Octavia wasn't making anything up. Her homegirl Philly really was always broke from paying her man's child support. He had like five kids and owed hundreds of thousands of dollars. If he didn't pay they'd lock him up. Octavia always had the energy of, *Let 'em*. Philly had told Octavia not to say anything, but she'd confessed she'd met her man while he was trying to break into her apartment. That was back when she lived at that complex that ended up getting condemned because the rats had taken over the entire first floor and wouldn't get scared if you fake-pumped like you were going to kick at them. Everything at that complex was falling apart. You could easily go up to any apartment door and just kick at the lock and it'd fly open. So that's what Philly's man Demarcus had done. She was sitting right in her living room watching *Grey's Anatomy* and looked over and saw this man and she was beside herself with lust and delusions.

"I'm telling you, Ock, he is giving Morris Chestnut mixed with like…Benicio del Toro," Philly had told her over the phone at the time, creaming in her Apple Bottom Jeans.

"Who the fuck is Benicio del Toro?" Octavia looked it up on her phone and was flabbergasted. She literally gasped. Was this bitch mentally ill. She was sick; had to be.

"Girl," Octavia had said, and she tried to be careful.

It was true back in college Philly had had a mental breakdown when she tried to join that sorority and they declined because she already had post-breastfeeding titties when she was only eighteen. Octavia at the time didn't think of it as a mental health sort of situation. Anyone'd have a breakdown over some shit like that.

They rejected her in front of everyone at the little sorority party they were having. They'd put a bowling alley in the front room at the house and so there'd been people in the background loudly bowling while Philly got dragged by one of the head sorority girls. Apparently the girl'd reached over and kind of flicked at the underside of one of Philly's titties and Philly, years later, had said that was really what sent her over the edge. She said it's why she just gave in and decided to have like three baby daddies. Before that, she'd vowed not to turn out like so many women she'd grown up with in her hometown. She'd go to college, graduate, and wouldn't have kids until she became a doctor and had found a partner with whom she could co-parent efficiently. Octavia felt like she didn't turn out too bad. She was a nurse with three ugly kids but they were in smart classes at school and all their dads paid child support, even the one who wore those Steve Harvey suits and worked at the T-Mobile kiosk at Garden Carcass Mall that was half-condemned and no one went there except to get Auntie Anne's because that was the only place you could get it.

Still, Philly had been unable to escape becoming a basic bird, like the pigeons and seahawks from her hometown. Like, one time she went out on a date with OJ Simpson. Just a coffee date, because he said he needed to make sure he liked her, thought she was attractive enough to want to eat her ass. *"I'm not paying thirty dollars for a plate at Applebee's if those titties aint sittin' right. Period."*. So that was a bust.

Octavia had been quiet on the phone for a long while.

"Ock!" Philly called, making sure Octavia hadn't passed away on her end.

Octavia was thinking how Philly had tried to explain away Demarcus breaking into people's homes as a career by comparing him to the folk hero Robin Hood. But Demarcus was no Robin Hood. He stole from bitches broke as him. Why couldn't he go up to Wall Street and break into those penthouses? Philly aint have shit in her apartment at the time she "met" her man. Just that little TV to watch *Grey's Anatomy* and them bunkbeds for the kids. Demarcus bustin' in her apartment to steal the three dollars and Blistex she got in her pocketbook.

Octavia didn't say any of this, though. Instead she said, "This nigga named Demarcus…" Philly had a thing about names, even though her full name was Philanderia Jones. It was a terrible name, but there was levels to this shit, and Demarcus was way worse. You couldn't really brag to other bitches about your man when his name was Demarcus. Demarcus did this and Demarcus did that. It just didn't sound right. *Demarcus kissed me on the lips.* Like, gross, why?

Philly was silent on her end, thinking.

Octavia hoped it was working, but to be safe, she decided to add, "He probably got a ponytail, don't he?"

Octavia had wanted to ask if he had cornrows, but at that time, *she* had cornrows, so it wouldn't work for her to disparage a hairstyle she'd become synonymous with. It was her brand. Not so secretly she felt like she could rock cornrows, but a home-invader named Demarcus was already doing too much to begin with. Having cornrows was just the rotted cherry on top of the shit sundae. She felt. But she couldn't say. So she changed it to ponytail last minute. It was a possibility. One of Philly's baby daddies was a lightskin man with a bright red afro ponytail and he looked like a complete piece of shit. He was her worst baby daddy by far. He looked like a damn clown. Like, literally. He worked in insurance sales.

Octavia knew Philly didn't fuck with ponytails.

"Well, it's low at the base of his head.." Philly had started to explain.

"Oh…" Octavia was speechless.

"It's not like Red's ponytail that's in the middle of his head." Red was what her lightskin baby daddy told everyone to call him. He acted like that was his nickname but it wasn't. His real name was Ellworth and no one called him anything because he was anti-human in his spirit and always smelled like gasoline. Octavia could never tell if it was the hair grease he used or was it coming from his body, his underarms or something. Either way, he was demonic.

Anyway, that was ten years ago, and Philly had kept up with Demarcus ever since. He moved in to her spot right away. Or, he never left after breaking in. He constantly cheated on her with bitches he met at the Y where he worked as a "personal trainer". Philly acted like she didn't know because occasionally he picked her ugly kids up from school or band practice or whatever. She acted like he was the best she could do. Octavia never agreed, but as of late she had started to suspect, maybe that was the case. If Philly could do better, wouldn't she?

Octavia thought how Philly actively fucked two different men with ponytails. One with an up ponytail and one with a down ponytail. All this time Octavia thought Philly had some sense. She knew to turn her nose up at the ponytail men. But if that were the case, why did she have two ponytail men as her mans? All up in her bed and pussy? Was she mental? Retarded? Clearly this girl didn't have all her marbles. Not one but *two* ponytail men!

The publisher said, "I'll see about additional Grey Butt Bus tickets. How many...*homegirls* are you thinking?"

Octavia thought about it. Well, one, Philly. Philly was always desperate to get out of her apartment with all them damn kids and that Demarcus. Philly's kids weren't bad. They were well behaved quiet little freaks. They did shit like science fair projects quietly in their room. But still they were there, you could sense them. And the apartment was small. The girl child had to have her own room because she threatened to call child services if she didn't get one, so there was no place for Philly to have like a little office or mom cave to herself, like she'd planned when they first moved to the new place. Octavia had thought what do you need an office for? Philly was a nurse. She did her work at the hospital. And there was no take home. She was just like putting IV bags into arms and stuff.

Octavia def thought it was a cooler job than driving a bunch of diseased children around all day and having to do gig jobs in between because driving a bus don't pay anything. But it wasn't an I-need-a-home-office type of job. Philly was always acting delusional like she was some sort of entrepreneur because she was a traveling nurse, but she only worked hospitals in the state they lived in. It's not like she was flying out to Abu Dhabi to administer drugs and apply gauze over there. And even if she was, how would a home office help in that effort? The mom cave idea was less cringe, but at the same time, no one told you to have three kids. And if one of them threatens to call child services, you dare them to do it and see if they have the balls. That's how Octavia's grandma and them would do. But Philly was the new generation. If your child threatens to call CPS, you quickly give in to their demands. Octavia just felt embarrassed for Philly because her daughter was her ugliest child by far and was supposed to be vulnerable to getting walked over and mistreated, but she was the queen over there. Even Demarcus was afraid of her, all in the groupchat talking about *"Dasani has black eyes. Black eyes like a shark. When she looks at me I see a dull, placid, seeping rage sitting patiently within, waiting. She will do something to me."*. Philly would always respond to these types of comments with laughing memes and emojis. Dasani was pretty terrifying, but it was funny that Demarcus was afraid, and secretly also funny that Philly couldn't have her "home office" or mom cave. That was the funniest, actually. Philly was the one they all secretly lowkey despised in the gang. There always had to be one and Philly was the one. At least she didn't have HIV like Nic.

Nic'd be ticket two, or three, if you added it to Octavia's ticket. Octavia had met Nic during her brief stint pretending to be a pleasant person and "team player", serving grinded-up chicken knuckles with a smile at Buffalo Wild Wings. Octavia had tried a million and one retail jobs and always got fired cuz she was big and brolic looking. Had a mean face even though her general attitude was fairly neutral. She never yelled or got reckless, unless you tried it with her, which didn't happen too often once she entered adulthood and her jiggly fat turned into more of a solid, hard mass. And especially she had no problems when she entered her cornrows and Timbs era. No problems at all. Though she hadn't liked the excessively aggressive energy she was giving off during that time. She never really rolled up on anyone. She'd stomp hard on people's feet on the bus and subway when she needed to, but that was about it. She wasn't really go-out-of-her-way rude, but she wasn't happy-smiley-face-we-are-all-god's-children nice, either. That wasn't acceptable enough for customer service. You had to put on a whole production. You couldn't even get away with shit if you were super pretty. Nic had been the prettiest when Octavia worked at Buffalo

Wild Wings and she'd get as many write-ups as Octavia for "looking like you don't want to be here".

"Of course I don't want to fucking be here!" Nic had yelled to one of their mush-brained managers after getting reprimanded for the fiftieth billion time for simply not standing around smiling like some lunatic.

Nic had a super-girly, Barbie doll sort of look that everyone seemed to be drawn to. When she first started at Buffalo Wild Wings Octavia had been a bit jealous, thinking if she looked like that, the manager wouldn't constantly be on her ass about implanting a permanent glassy-eyed grin on her face as if she'd just undergone a lobotomy. Nic would get away with have a resting bitch face, which she had, because she was thin with big tatas and a pretty face, even with a small amount of makeup, which she was told to tone down at the end of her first week, but Octavia just thought it was because one of their main managers was a man-looking woman who was going bald at the top of her head. The mannish manager's hair was both like straw and worms. She was jealous. But then Nic started getting shit from the rest of the managers, who were all thirsty ass men. And you could tell they were attracted to her and got excited when she gave them attention, but if only she would smile more.

Nic wasn't having it. Anytime she was approached to be reprimanded she'd make a whole scene. You could tell she thought it'd embarrass the managers if she yelled so the customers could hear, but it just caused them to double down. She was getting written-up every day at one point, and then eventually fired after so many. Octavia stupidly quit in solidarity, thinking it would get her some pussy, but Nic had laughed when Octavia tried to make a move. *"Oh no, girl, I'm strictly-dickly!"*, like it was cute to be straight. It wasn't, and Octavia had been secretly glad when, later on, after Octavia had long been rusted-shut into her imprisonment at Friendzone Penitentiary, Nic had to call the gang over to her crib and have that big dramatic moment where she "revealed" her positive HIV status while handing out roast beef cranberry sandwiches from Quiznos.

“I'm pretty sure it's from Jerome,” Nic had said. At the time, she was dating somebody's baby father. Actually multiple somebodys' baby father. She had met him at the job she took after getting canned from Buffalo Wild Wings. Lady Footlocker. She got fired from there quickly too for getting into an entanglement with Jerome. Apparently his “main” was one of the managers over there. At that point, it had become clear to Octavia that Nic was a bird. Octavia had always dumbly thought if you were hot, good looking, had both of your arms (Octavia had lost an arm during middle school when she tried to pull that karate shit during a street fight she got into when she went to visit her cousins in the hood. She had a wood arm now that worked well enough. She only needed one good arm to drive her bus and write her 9/11 erotica)--Octavia thought if you were attractive and everyone agreed with your appearance, then they agreed with your presence, and you were as good as gold. Octavia knew from growing up fat with a moustache, and then later with no arm, and then after that she had an arm but it was made out of a fucking lincoln log--She knew that most people were shallow. It was fine, not a big deal. She was, too. If Octavia was one of them fine ass lesbians like Alicia Keys she would be moving real reckless. She'd straight up be a serial killer and sincerely feel like she wouldn't even go to jail because everyone would think well, she's attractive, and she gets a lot of pussy, so is it really all that serious? But really, being hot, fine, whatever - *that helps*, but it isn't some ultimate panacea or anything. Also, she'd noticed, sometimes it worked against you. Like, Nic was black, so being hot could be a weapon, but a lot of the times it just made her more intimidating to pretty much every group, and that made them hate her even more than if she'd been blessed to be born with a hunchback or one of her legs is like extremely bigger than the other.

Anyway, being attractive barely did anything for Nic. Her life was trash. And for Octavia, she realized she'd dumbly been believing that the hot girls were not only blessed with looks, but the brains to make their blessing work in their favor. Nic was a damb dummy and that clearly wasn't the case for her at all. Who the fuck works at--How do you even *find* a Lady Footlocker?? Octavia had thought this bitch was joking when she told her she worked there. She thought it was a joke from a damn movie or some shit! What the fuck is a Lady Footlocker?! Regular Footlocker has women shit!!

So Nic had met Jerome there. At this Lady Footlocker. Was fucking him in the backrooms. Octavia couldn't even imagine what they held in the backrooms of a Lady Footlocker. Did they sell douche kits with the Nike logo on them? Like what even was back there?..

"*Of course* you got AIDS from a nigga name Jerome you met at fucking Lady Foot Locker," Phulicia had said. Phulicia was Philly's younger sister who never had a man and she was very alone. Phulicia was pale-yellow, and tall like a basketball man. The only time she'd ever been in love was like fifteen years ago to a basehead named Breyer who always had mad dirt under his fingernails and a crispy, flat-ironed side-bang that never moved. She'd met him at a Fall Out Boy concert and hasn't met anyone she really wants to open her butt up and show her asshole to, ever since.

"It's not AIDS, it's <u>HIV</u>," Nic corrected. She didn't seem embarrassed enough for any of them. It was irritating.

"It's disgusting," Barb said, holding her purse close on her lap, like she thought a roach was gonna come slithering out from a crack in the wall of Nic's apartment and waltz over to lift her wallet.

Nic lived in the projects and it looked exactly like Cabrini-Green from *Candyman* except there were Amazon lockers out front but they'd been spray painted with gangster Looney Tunes characters. Except for the amazon locker tagged with gangster versions of Bugs and Tweety Bird, it looked exactly like the projects from *Candyman*. Ock thought it was worse because sexy, refined Candyman didn't haunt Nic's projects. Just some neighborhood-renowned child rapist named Lawerence whose mom worked at the post office and if you accused her son of leering at or harming your child she would withhold your packages.

“Ma,” Leece said, putting her hand on Barb’s arm. “This isn’t olden times. If someone got AIDS now you gotta pretend it’s all good.”

“Don’t touch me!” she screeched as sort of a general statement. Phulicia didn’t remove her hand from Barb’s arm. She did not take it as a general sort of note about Barb that applied to everyone. She assumed Barb meant it only for Nic. Everyone else decided that Barb meant it as a warning for the whole of humanity, but especially and most importantly, most urgently in the moment, for Nic, yes.

“They have done all sorts of research and things,” Nic was saying, and she really believed it. Nic was the type of person to start buying elderberry syrup and turmeric satchels from an online apothecary and decide that would basically take care of everything. She wasn’t even really a hippie type. She threw her trash in the street all the time and scoffed in elementary science class when it was suggested trees and plants provide oxygen to humans. She thought it was inappropriate and intrusive of them. She imagined trees quietly watching her, wishing to plunge their rough, splintery branches deep into her lungs and guts.

Barb said, “No amount of research in the world is gonna get me to pretend like I think having AIDS is okay.”

“Well, I don’t need your permission to be okay with existing,” Nic was saying as Phil, Amander’s husband, was correcting Barb that, again, Nic did not have full-blown AIDS, but the virus that could lead to auto-immune deficiency syndrome if left untreated, HIV.

Everyone rolled their eyes at Phil, even Nic, whom he’d attempted to defend.

Amander went to college with Ock and Philly. She was the only one of the college crew who had something to show for them bitch ass student loans. She had some unknowable, vaguely ominous, sort of corporate job where she made six figures a year and could afford to have some Dominican woman come to her house every week to blow out her hair and clean her three bathrooms. Amander was the only one of their crew with slave money. It was a bit of a sore spot. Philly, when it was just her and Ock, she'd go on and on about how she was a nurse and nurses made good money and were respected. Plus all her baby daddies paid their child support. She wasn't hurting for money. She'd upgraded from that rat-infested apartment and had gotten a townhouse with three rooms and it had a guest bathroom downstairs. Demarcus had a ton of dedicated clients at his YMCA trainer job. He was doing so well he was taking house calls and that was bringing in a nice income. *"Demarcus can afford Just For Me for his ponytail now so it's not all rough and scratchy-looking when he flat-irons it."*

Ock would just sit there listening to this shit, sick to her stomach. They were losers.

"Demarcus straightens his hair?" was all she could say in these delusional little meetings they'd conduct. "He told me his hair was naturally straight because his grandmother was Chickasaw Indian?"

Philly said, "She was. She committed several child murders on their reservation and was never arrested because the usual rules don't apply to them. Like, I think they have cops, but it's Indian cops so they only have bows and arrows and you only get the one shot.."

Ock just looked at her.

"Her name was Juanita," Philly went on. "Juanita Sims."

Ock just nodded. She wasn't like Philly, always having to convince herself that things were better than they actually were. Less sad as shit. Octavia had never really grown up with any discernible goals or desires. It wasn't something that came natural to her. When she looked back on like the first twelve years of her life, it's just a blur. Not because she experienced some absurd amount of trauma or anything. She'd not been abused to the point of no return, nor had she suffered any contusions to the brain. Had never been kicked in the head by a horse, as so often happens. It was just that for the first twelve years of Octavia's life she was literally a blob. She had mostly no thoughts. When she tried to recall the time she could remember only ever caring about what snacks she'd get to have for the day. Her grandmother was keen on oatmeal creme pies and these little strawberry shortcake rolls she'd get from the little mart around the corner from their house. Octavia wasn't allowed to have more than one snack a day, so most of her day during her growing years revolved around stressing over how she'd be able to sneak more than her allotted amount. And occasionally Octavia would be denied a snack entirely, due to arbitrary sorts of things her grandmother would get upset over. Some dust on the top of the TV set; or an errant shoe out of place. Octavia would be "banned" from the snack cabinet. Which after a certain point stopped mattering because Octavia had learned to create an emergency stash for just these moments.

After Octavia's best friend in eighth grade Ariel was murdered by her father during a nasty custody battle between him and her mother, who worked at the local veterinary clinic and was known for being super overzealous about putting down people's pets, always pushing for it–After that, Octavia started to think about what she wanted to do next. She felt a vague emptiness that she vaguely understood needed to be filled. She thought about getting a new best friend, but Ariel had been acquired on accident. Ariel had sat down next to her one day in sixth grade and just started chatting away whilst Octavia sat at her desk, lumplike, and stared ahead at their English teacher droning away about a gang of greaser twinks from olden times.

Ariel was strange. Her race was non discernible. Her face didn't make sense, the way it was set up. She looked like a cartoon, not totally human. She had a gigantic head almost like an abnormal growth more than a human head. She had a pale-pink face littered with freckles. And not the cute kind of freckles. The kind where it looks like someone sneezed hard into your face a nose full of blood. She was always smiling and laughing even when no one was talking. She could never sit still for more than a few moments. She had this wild mane of fuzzy clown hair that sat on her head as if she'd been electrocuted. She looked like a mental patient. Ariel came across like she'd been dropped down from somewhere instead of being born normal from a human womb like everyone else. When she got murdered, Octavia wasn't even surprised. Her existence definitely came across like a mistake, and it appeared the universe had corrected the error. Still, Octavia liked her. She never made fun of Octavia's moustache or told her that two chocolate milks at lunch was two chocolate milks too many. Plus she always had some interesting things to talk about. Octavia learned about foot in mouth disease from Ariel.

After she was gone, Octavia was kinda bored. Getting a new friend wasn't really an option though because Ariel had been a fluke. Octavia wouldn't come upon people just going up to her and making her their friend again until college, when she met Philly and Mander. Before them, Ock had sort of just floated. She merely considered thinking about maybe getting around to doing something, anything. She got lucky in that she was smart. Or, that she was afraid of getting a whoopin' from her grandmother if she brought home a bad report card. So she got good grades. Then her high school guidance counselor, who suspected Octavia was possibly retarded–but like, one of them idiot savant type of retards–had pushed for Octavia to apply for college, which was not anything she had really considered. By that point she'd gotten a job at KFC because it was where she ate most of her meals. She had sort of vaguely decided to maybe just keep on there and become manager or head mashed potato maker. But she got accepted into college, which was weird. She hadn't really wanted to go, but the guidance counselor had made it seem a whole world would be opened up to Octavia if she attended, and they were paying for most of the tuition through scholarships, so she carried on there. Just floating, floating.

She had no major in school and couldn't recall anything she was studying or working on, but she'd made two friends, much in the same way she'd befriended Ariel, which was not at all. They just took her on and Octavia did not protest. Philly had been assigned to be Octavia's roommate. On move-in day, Philly was wearing some sort of church wig and a jean vest and jean skirt. Later, Octavia would learn this was what Philly considered "business casual". She was always "dressing up" for random non-events. Move-in day; her son's kindergarten graduation; when she goes to the DMV to update her license. Always a strange older lady wig that sits atop her head like a bird, and always some sort of churchish type of skirt, with matching vest. It was impressive that she'd managed to find three different men to cum raw inside her. Octavia knew men would fuck anything. They'd fuck Woody from *Toy Story*, and he has no ass. But still.

Philly had all sorts of rules for Octavia on move-in day. She had printed out literally a list of instructions and directives. At first Octavia thought it was something their RA had typed up for everyone on the floor, but when Octavia looked at the list, it said, *"Authored by Philanderia G. Jones"* (The G stood for Geraldine, because of course).

Such "rules" included:

- "No zebra print" (Octavia thought this was strange as Philly certainly seemed like a Little Miss Zebra Print sort, and, when she looked over Philly's shoulder to where her bed was, she spotted a leopard print comforter and cheetah print bed sheets and pillow cases. Octavia wasn't familiar with animal print culture, so it all seemed like the same shit to her. Zebras, cheetahs; lions, tigers and bears. Octavia decided her roommate was severely mentally ill. She nodded and smiled so as not to be assassinated in her sleep.)
- "No Otis Redding after midnight" (What the fuck is Otis Redding. Octavia decided it was some sort of slang for marijuana. Octavia didn't do weed. She was too shy.)
- "No talking about any international trips you have taken or may take in the future. I haven't been anywhere and don't want to hear it." (Octavia had no issue with this rule)
- "No using my printer - the ink is expensive and I am on a fixed income" (This rule inspired anxiety in Octavia. Would they need to be printing shit? For what - which course?? Octavia had never used a printer in her life. She thought it was just in movies. Her stomach hurt worrying over this. It was one of those moments when you realize

everyone knows something but you. It was like that time when she realized dinosaurs were apparently real. Like, they actually existed. She thought it was like dragons and was only in fantasy books. She had spoken confidently to their fantastical nature many a time and no one had corrected her. She felt sick.)

- "No having sex in the room. It's gross. No I won't leave so you can give a blowjob to some musty ass Engineering major. You're not putting a fucking sock on the doorknob - get a fucking single." (They had Engineer at their school? Octavia wondered what her major would be? She couldn't think of anything she was interested in. At one point it'd been dinosaurs, until she understood they weren't just characters in a picture book and were actually some real life giant shits that could literally step on her by a mistake and she'd be extra fucking dead forever. At present, she had no interests. She liked to eat, but did not want to get a degree in Cooking. Was that a degree? She knew Eating wasn't, because she'd looked it up. As a joke mostly, but a little bit she was serious.)

Ock and Philly became fast friends by virtue of proximity. Philly had tried to branch out - joining the sorority and asking gals from her classes out for milkshakes and things, but she got no takers. She was too bossy and not smart or hot enough for people to let it slide. So she was stuck with Octavia.

With Mander, she was dark and quiet; shy-passing. She was quite bookish and nerdy. Always in the library being a huge loser. She and Octavia had only become friends because they'd been assigned a project together for one of their Psychology classes. Randomly Octavia had decided to pursue a degree in Social Work. She thought it'd be fun to work for CPS and take people's kids away, realizing later she was just trying to act out some fantasy she'd had as a child of a CPS angel coming to rescue her from her grandmother. She did not want to wash her dry, tight feet in a basin and then apply globs of Jergens lotion to their dinosaur-like form on a nightly basis. She wanted to be a normal child. She wanted to be in her room designing up plans on how she was going to come into school and kill all the kids in her class. She figured those free-spirited school shooter kids had all the time in the world for jotting up manifestos and buying trench coats and things. And disposable income! Guns and trench coats and paper to write manifestos on weren't cheap! Octavia's "allowance" was fifty cents a week. It was her "pay" for cleaning the toilets and scrubbing her grandmother's back in the tub every Sunday, Wednesday and Friday. What the fuck are you supposed to buy with fifty cents? Even back then you could barely buy gum. And Octavia did not bother with anything you couldn't swallow, so what the fuck.

Working together on their project, Amander would confess things to Octavia. She told Octavia she hated her roommate and would stand over her bed at night staring at her sleeping form, deciding.

Octavia was curious. "Deciding what?"

Amander shrugged, very casually. She was always wearing these fuzzy, oversized sweaters. Octavia thought it was to hide her boobs. They were huge Triple HHH great aunt type of titties.

"What I'm going to do," Amander said. "Whether I'll kill her, or maybe do something less heavy, but more intimate, like spit on her eyelid. Or, let spit dribble from my mouth onto her eyelid. I wouldn't actually" and here she mimed violently hawking a loogie.

Another nod and smile scenario. Octavia was too curious, though, and carried on with questioning.

"You'd kill?" she asked wide-eyed and dull, like some retarded toddler.

Amander kind of shook it off like it was nothing. "It depends."

Octavia leaned forward, inappropriately fascinated, she could feel, even in the moment. "Depends on what?"

"If it's warranted."

Octavia thought for a moment, then asked, "Has your roommate done anything?"

"She exists," Amander laughed, and she seemed completely deranged. She added, "But no, seriously - she ate like all of my pretzels. I never said she could."

"Couldn't you talk to her about it?" Octavia offered, still so naive, so dumb.

Amander turned a dark eye upon her. "I shouldn't have to."

Octavia converted back to nod and smile mode. *Of course*, she made her polite, appeasing smile express. Scared, she tried to join on with Amander.

"My roommate is annoying, too," she said. At this point, she was fine with Philly. Octavia liked how Philly would always come home to their dorm looking busted and beat down. Mascara streaming down her caked-up face; her long jean skirt all twisted up. Her jean vest in tatters. She was always having some scuffle with some man she was dating. She had acted so prissy about copulation but stayed getting her back blown out. And she picked like the shittiest guys she could find. At minimum, every one of her paramours had at least a little bit of an STD. Philly would express relief and glee if a guy "only" had chlamydia. If Philly went a few weeks with no sores or scratching, she considered herself "on the come up". She was a trainwreck, and Octavia was grateful to have front row seats.

"Yeah, how?" Amander said, so Octavia had to throw bestie under the bus.

"She's like, *always* having sex."

This really shocked Amander, whom Octavia had already taken as a full-on serial killer. She was impressed with herself for getting a reaction out of basically the Zodiac's protege.

"In your room?" Amander said, eyes wide with disgust and then there was a slight glint of murderous rage. Octavia felt she was developing murderous designs.

Octavia nodded violently, snapping her neck so hard it made a cracking sound.

"YES!" she lied. Philly never brought her men to the room. It was one of the rules.

"What a disgusting bitch," Amander decided, then, almost bright, "You should kill her."

Octavia shut it down quickly, shaking her head, "Too shy."

This appeased Amander. She looked at Octavia for a moment, as if sizing her up, and decided with pity that she agreed.

"Well, anyway," she said. "It's not for everyone. I haven't done it."

Octavia was both relieved and disappointed. That was when she thought Amander was "cool". Octavia thought Amander to be very strange and intense and eerie and that all seemed very cool to her. But then Amander started dating Phil, her first boyfriend. And Octavia could barely contain her disgust.

Amander had met Phil during her study abroad year in France. Phil was there doing his study abroad for the school he went to. They met at McDonald's. They both hated France and the study abroad program. Amander thought her host family was "musty", and Phil thought his host family "hated blacks". Upon meeting Phil, and hearing the origin story of their relationship, Octavia felt like she'd too be racist if one of the primary black people she was being exposed to was the likes of Phil.

Phil's hairline started in the middle of his scalp at the crown of his head. And this was back when they were in their early twenties. It wasn't receding, it was just like that when he was born. And not only that, he wore his hair in a short afro style. Sometimes the afro was "rounded" and sometimes he'd let it be wild and fuzzy. Octavia couldn't tell which was worse. He looked like that midget man from *The Jeffersons*, except not hot.

Phil had a strange, incomprehensible sort of body. He was the height of a semi-tall woman. The same height as Amander who was tall for a girl, at 5'9". But short for a man.

He had very long arms; arms that looked too long like they were separated from their sockets and just hanging there useless. He had one of those skinny-fat sort of bodies. Thin in most places but had a confounding triple chin hanging beneath his jowls, and a rounded stomach that made him look like he was pregnant with worms. He looked like one of those starving kids from the commercials with the flies on their face. Except Octavia knew for a fact that Phil ate Quiznos every day because once he'd started up with Amander they were always, all three, and then sometimes Philly, having to hang out together, and every time they ended up at Quiznos. Phil <u>had</u> to have Quiznos, it was like an addiction. Breakfast, lunch, and dinner - he stayed at Quiznos. He smelled like Quiznos. His body looked like the Q in Quiznos.

When Nic had made her HIV announcement, Phil was saying, "Well, I know what I'm talking about. I have a degree in Biomedics from Oakland University."

"What the fuck is Oakland University?" Leece inquired.

Octavia said, "I thought your degree was in Poetry?", which she regretted. Phil was a writer like her, but he didn't act shameful about it like is expected when a grown adult decides to spend time making up stories and they're being totally dead ass serious. Phil tried to make his living as a writer, and most of his writing was poetry, which isn't a thing anyone is interested in, ever. He also was the Soup Reviewer for something called the *Senior Citizen Gazette*. He reviewed soups, and then wrote a column about it and was paid, not considerably, Octavia was sure. Pretty much everything Phil had going on sounded made up. He wasn't a real person. His name was Phil, for christ's sake.

Phil looked at Octavia with a swelling love in his eyes. More than anything, he craved being asked about his work. Tearing up slightly, he said, "I triple-majored in Biomedics, Poetry, and Slam Poetry. Initially it was a double major: biomedics and poetry, with slam poetry being umbrellaed under Poetry, but by the time I was to graduate, Slam Poetry had been sectioned off into its own specialty."

"As it should be," Barb said sarcastically. Phil never knew she was being sarcastic because she was older and she wouldn't put an inflection in her voice to make it clear she was making fun of him.

Phil nodded with admiration at her as Leece was saying with disgust, "What the fuck is Biomedics?"

As it stood, Octavia thought, she would need…around eight Grey Butt Bus tickets for her trip to Florida. One for her. Two makes Philly. Three for Philly's little sister Leece because Leece never had a man and never had anywhere to go. Four makes Amander, and then five and six for Phil and their son Franklin. Amander brought them everywhere she went. They always had to do everything as a family. Everyone else in the crew wanted to complain but when they thought about it it's not like they were against the idea of family joining them on outings - Leece and Philly's mom was in their crew, and Octavia was always bringing her son to the club and when they'd go to the casino, because his dad was busy impregnating other bitches and didn't have time for him. So it's not like Amander's situation was unique - it's just they all hated Phil. He smelled like Vaseline. But he was very dry and had a sheen of ash on every exposed area of his skin, so he clearly didn't use it.

Ticket seven was for Barb, who went everywhere her daughters went, who were her best friends, even though she hated them and often talked about how she wished abortion was more readily available to her at the time of her being pregnant with them as if she'd been with child during Civil War Times and not in the 1970s…

Ticket eight was for Octavian, Octavia's son. His dad had already texted her talkin bout *"I shot the club up in this chola broad and now she got the Latin Kings on me cuz I won't give her my prepaid debit card to go down 2 the chokey to wash my son out her guts"*. Octavia didn't know what any of those words were. She knew them separately, but put together, it did not mean anything to her, but she could guess his nigganese, and assumed he wouldn't be available to watch Octavian while she was off reading her Anne Frank erotica at the Gator Gunk Gas Station, Grill, and Book Room/Rest Stop.

—

As Octavia was finishing up in the handicap stall (she is able bodied she just prefers the spacious quarters) in the bathroom at the back of the Obese Auntware department in Macy's in the basement, she heard coming from the front of the bathroom, by the sinks, "*I will tear your life apart, Eileen.* I will take your head off with a sword and put it on the floor like a soccer ball and kick it hard into the trees."

"Well, I'm reporting you to the manager," Octavia heard a feeble old white lady voice reply. Eileen, presumably.

Octavia went up close to the door of her stall, very sneaky-like, and she put her face up to the little open bit at the sides of the door to try to look upon the scene. She couldn't see Eileen, as she seemed to be standing by the entrance door to the bathroom, which was obscured by some random structure jutting out from the wall. The entrance door to the bathroom seemed to demand more privacy than any of the actual stalls. It was a mystery who was entering the bathroom, but then once they were fully inside, in a stall, the mystery was all gone away. Everything would be known about every occupant of the bathroom. How they looked, smelled - every private thought would be discerned from each audible groan or tinkle of piss.

The non-Eileen one was saying, in a low growl, "I will kick your head off into the moon."

"You keep doing this," Eileen was saying in a shaky old-timey sort of voice. "You keep these threats up, and I keep reporting you. I tell Miguel, one day, you'll kill us all. But he doesn't understand English because he swam over here from Mexico." (Eileen said "Mexico" like "Meh-gee-koh" - Octavia had never heard anyone say it like that and was impressed.)

"This is exactly why Miguel's the boss," the non-Eileen one was saying. "They swim over here and they're confident, because you know what: I'm not fucking swimming from one end of a kiddie pool to the other. I almost drowned in one just last week. I was babysitting my nephew, Donnie. He's still in the hospital but I'm fine because I'm an adult and not going to actually fucking almost drown in a kiddie pool, do you know what I mean?"

Octavia, from her stall, could hear Eileen nod her head. Octavia didn't know why she could hear the old woman's head actually nodding. Octavia realized in that moment that she didn't think she'd ever heard the actual action of head nodding. She never considered the action was typically accompanied with sound effects. She was quite sure, in fact, that it typically wasn't. Octavia guessed the old woman was wearing a wig, or had some sort of weird non-comprehensible old timey disease like Maurfin's syndrome or something. Something weird. Rickets in the neck? Old timey cricket neck disease or something. Ol' timey head crinkle noise syndrome or some such.

"They get over here," non-Eileen went on, "and they're feeling themselves because they were able to swim over from whatever hellhole they came from and now they're all confident and shit."

Octavia could hear Eileen nodding again. It sounded like someone was crumbling a bag of potato chips.

Eileen said, "Well, that's why I told them to put up the borders."

Octavia, from her little slit, could see the non-Eileen one turn up her face. She was dry-looking and had a crumpled body like a worn-out, overstuffed Futon. She was humpbacked and it looked like both a disability and a suit of armor. She said, in a low, accusatory sort of voice, "You don't know anyone who can take care of that."

Eileen got all hot and indignant, "I know a priest, who knows the pope!"

The non-Eileen straightened up as much as her humpback would allow, crossed her arms, and looked down upon Eileen, "You know a child molester who knows the Supreme Child Molester."

Eileen was saying in a breathless panic how she was going to report non-Eileen to Miguel during the middle of non-Eileen going "Wow!" in a super fake, cheery voice and her face was wide and happy and her eyes were black and hard and dead.

"Wowww!" she threatened in a sing-songy voice as Eileen double-downed on her promise to report non-Eileen to this Miguel whichever or whoever.

"Yeah, good luck translating that into espanol," non-Eileen called after a huffily retreating Eileen.

When Eileen was completely gone Octavia watched as non-Eileen looked off into some unknowable area in the bathroom, smiling, her eyes still and dead. She seemed very satisfied with herself. After a while, Octavia felt a chill. She wondered why the woman continued to stand in the middle of the bathroom, staring off with her arms crossed grinning stupidly, eerily, at nothing. Then, as if flicked on randomly, Octavia saw the woman's eyes glint over to where she stood in her stall. Octavia realized she could be seen standing right up close to the door with her face pressed against the open slit.

Octavia hadn't really paid attention to the woman when she walked into the bathroom. Really she had sort of…thundered into the bathroom, holding her bottom closed with her foot-long, alligator-skin LesbianPlus wallet to keep her poop in. She didn't really have control over her bowels or anal sphincter.

She had bum rushed into the bathroom, and she couldn't remember if she had shouted or had grumbled, *"Move, I gotta booboo!"*, but she did remember no one had been in her way. The woman had been standing by the sink, quite out of the way, and aside from her, the bathroom was empty.

So she hadn't the mental capacity at the time, with her lunch from Taco Bell turtling itself with great speed from her intestines, to notice that the woman, non-Eileen, had a little set-up by the sink. She was standing at the front of the sink, and next to her, on the counter, were a sad set of what looked like hand towels, and beside them a basket that looked like it was full of an assortment of hand soaps and mini shampoos stolen from motels in the surrounding areas. Octavia was too far away to really see, but one of the soaps looked like the clam soap from a Honeymoon Motel in the area she visited once to do sex with an old girlfriend of hers. The girlfriend had a roommate and the roommate was against homosexual sex and threatened to call the anti-gay police on Octavia's girlfriend if she brought any of her lady lovers into the home. Octavia had wanted to say that there wasn't any such thing as anti-gay police, but she actually wasn't entirely sure. It actually sounded maybe real? So she said nothing. They had clam-shaped bottles of lotion at the motel. Also a racoon was living in their room's bathroom so they didn't go in there because they were scared and the racoon seemed not to be.

"You, in there!" a voice called. The voice belonged to the non-Eileen one. Octavia pressed her face up hard against the door to get a better look, but the back of her body she pushed away so her feet wouldn't show under the door, the diabetic nurse shoes with the velcro straps she wore mostly for comfort but also because of the ghastly squeaking noise they made when she walked. She liked the noise, the idea she had of irritating people whenever she walked into a room. The only time she didn't like it was when she had to rush into a public bathroom with shit almost sloughing out of her ass. She didn't feel like the squeaks helped with her brief embarrassment in the moment, though she did think it was a plus for intimidation. She knew in these moments she came across like a deranged homeless. That day, there had been no one in the way, but if there had been, they would've moved with ease just at the sound of the hurried, heavy squeaks.

The woman walked up to Octavia's stall door and looked at the door as if she expected it to open up and Narnia would be on the other side. She didn't seem excited for Narnia, but kind of like she felt if Narnia was on the other side it'd be something to do. She'd walk in and look around and maybe talk to a goblin or whatever the fuck they had over there, but she wasn't like, a stan of the idea.

The woman put her face to eye level with where Octavia had been peering from.

"You, in there," she said again, but it was more of a question this time. Her voice was clear and booming like an old timey radio announcer. She didn't look old timey, though. She was in her fifties, maybe. Octavia at one point would have thought fifties to be old timey but she was only four years away from being in that category and she still barely knew how to tie her shoes, so being fifty no longer felt as corpse-adjacent as she had once thought it to be.

Octavia, sweating from the neck now, continued to peer back at the woman.

"Do you need assistance?" the woman said.

Octavia wondered why she was being spoken to through a stall door. It suddenly came to her how odd it was to be accosted whilst occupying the lavatory. Who does that? Octavia could see if maybe she had thudded to the floor and was moaning. Maybe then it'd make sense to be getting spoken to by someone on the other side of the door, but that hadn't happened. Sure, the woman could see Octavia standing up by the door and peering out strangely, but that was none of her business, really. Octavia wondered what business the woman did have in the lavatory, but felt she couldn't ask because then the woman would feel entitled to asking Octavia back her own question, for which she did not have a satisfying, non-sus response.

Octavia kept staring out through the slit in the door.

The woman said, "Are you experiencing gastrointestinal distress?". She waited. When she did not receive an immediate response, she added,

"When you entered the bathroom I noticed you were tumescent with feces. You glowed with excrement."

Octavia didn't like people looking at her when she was in the bathroom. *Turn away*, she thought.

"Don't notice shit I'm doin–Don't notice how I look when I'm bussin' in the bathroom," Octavia spoke at last to the strange figure. "Don't notice me tumescent with shit. Everyone comin' up in here tumescent with shit or piss. Aint nothin' new."

Octavia was annoyed, and she wanted nachos and also chicken noodle soup. She decided to get this for her second lunch once she was able to escape.

"Oh, naturally," the woman sort of chortled, and then she pulled slightly away from the door. She looked like a vampire. Like a real one, not a glittery one. Like one that for real will suck out all your blood on some weirdo shit. She had a widow's peak and gave the impression of like Dracula's illegitimate mixed raced secret shame. Her skin had the pallor of ash. She looks like Phil, Octavia thought, and she shuddered. At least this figure had a hairline, but secretly it was worse because of the widow's peak. When Octavia looked at it it made her itch. She felt sick and like she wanted to scream.

Instead though she said, accidentally with a shaky voice, "What do you want? Is there something you want?"

The woman looked at her. She said, "I'd ask the same of you."

Octavia sucked her teeth and moved to unlock and then swing open the door to the handicapped stall. She'd had enough. She was no longer going to stand. She was going to sit. She walked from the stall to the sink and tried to sit on it but it was too high and quickly she was out of breath from the effort of trying to hop on. The GirlPlus MissBig-sized FUBU jeans she was wearing had started to slide off her bum and expose her ass crack. She noticed the woman glance in the direction of her ass, and her gaze lingered a bit. Octavia didn't think she was a fellow pussy licker, she thought the woman had some sort of big bitch asscrack fetish, which was a totally different thing altogether.

The woman said to Octavia, who was out of breath from trying to hop up on the counter, "How'd it go?"

Octavia looked at her, breathing hard and heavy, her eyelids drooping with exhaustion. She didn't say anything. She wondered if she was to be murdered. This'd be the perfect place. The basement of Macy's in the Obese Auntware department. No one would ever find her or know. No one would hear her screams. Well, maybe some of the Obese Auntware shoppers. But would they come running? Certainly not.

I'm done for, she thought, in a voice not her own. She would never say those words.

"Did you complete?" the woman pressed. Octavia noticed she was wearing a nametag. *Mary*.

"Sometimes I go to the bathroom and I don't complete, and I don't know what to do. I've heard of people reaching up into their anal cavities to relieve themselves, but I think that's only for a certain type of folk. Demented sorts. Homosexuals."

She eyed Octavia in a targeted sense.

Catching her breath, but still vaguely incapacitated, Octavia managed, "You work here? At Macy's?"

A strange flash of disgust sheathed over Mary's grey face. She looked like she had sniffed a great big pile of dinosaur dung.

“I work in this *bathroom*,” she spat. She said “bathroom” in a super drawn-out intense way. She made it have like three extra syllables.

Octavia glanced over at the sad pile of hand towels and the basket of stolen soaps.

“You’re a bathroom attendant?”

“What does it look like?” Mary said with irritation, looking away from Octavia as someone new entered the room.

It was a great big white woman and she was a huffin’ and puffin’.

Octavia took time to wonder why bathroom attendant existed as a job? Was it a troll? And what non-disabled in the brain person would even apply for the job? You’re meant to stand up in a room full of shit smells all day and be fine with it because you’re getting like fifty dollars or whatever at the end of your shift? Octavia wondered if she was being too judgmental. She drove a bus, after all. That’s a job a deranged teacher has on a cartoon TV show. It wasn’t a job for a real-life human being. Also Octavia wondered if maybe the job paid more than she thought. She assumed basic slave wages, but maybe it was viewed more as a specialized profession and demanded big beaucoup buckaroos.

“Hey, don’t come in here, bitch!” Mary shouted at the big white woman who had yet to reach a stall of her choice. She had stopped by the entrance and set down all her shopping bags. Octavia could then see she was pulling out what looked like a rotisserie chicken meal from a bag labeled “Boston Market”.

Octavia wondered if she got that from the food court in the mall. It became her immediate next goal.

From one of her bags the big white woman pulled out a beach chair. She unfolded it and started setting it up.

Mary jerked her face to Octavia with her jaw hanging open in a comical fashion. Octavia snorted at the sight, and snot came out of her nose. Mary stared at it for a moment, then snatched her ashen face back in the direction of Miss Big Boston Market.

“This isn’t a cafeteria!” Mary reminded the woman.

When the woman spoke she had an almost cliche sort of deep, hokey, trailer park sub-creature sort of voice. She seemed both slow and kind of sexy. Her teeth were grey and brown and shiny with some sort of slime. Maybe slime like that of old deli meat.

“I ain’ goin’ alldaway tew no cafeteria,” she drawled, then splatted heavily down onto her chair and it broke and she did not react at all to it being broke. It appeared she could not feel the seat broken under her fat.

Octavia felt a panic, because now it seemed the woman had not purchased the Boston Market from the Food Court. She would go on a killing spree if she walked all the way over there and Boston Market wasn’t one of the options. She would become the Joker.

Octavia thought about how she had only come into Macy’s to shop for her upcoming book tour. She had asked her publisher how to dress for Florida.

“I’m not sure if there is clothes there,” the publisher said and it inspired Octavia to question this broad’s professionalism. Shouldn’t she, as a publisher, have a more concrete answer?

The publisher said, “Well, I’m still moanly just making sandwiches at the Quiznos, if you remember.”

“What is moanly?” Octavia attempted to bring the conversation back to Earth, back to sense.

“M-mainly,” the publisher slurred. She seemed to be drunk, perhaps, or had done a stroke. Octavia didn’t want to ask because what if it were the latter? Then she’d have to offer condolences maybe? What do you say if someone has done a stroke? Do you say sorry? Octavia wasn’t good in these situations. One of the old crones she delivered to for meals-on-wheels once had used Octavia to rehearse talking about her recent anal cancer diagnosis. “Gross, what the fuck?” Octavia had said, and the woman reported her and Octavia had been suspended for three weeks no pay. Then there was another time, her second chance, when another meals-on-wheels idiot had told Octavia his eldest daughter had recently committed suicide. Octavia knew better now not to rejoin with a “Gross, what the fuck”. In this instance, she said “Aw” in like a fake sad sort of voice, and the man, with his milked-over eyes kind of just stared through her. Octavia considered he was reminiscing about his crackhead daughter. He hadn’t said she was a crackhead, but he *had* said her name was Jackie. Octavia imagined the woman having no teeth, or if she had teeth, they were black and few and far between. The man, after a while, seemed to be waiting for Octavia to go on, so she said, “Why…did…she….kill…herself?”, real slow like that, because she really hadn’t known what she was going to say once she’d opened her mouth, but once it was all said and done, she’d produced a complete sentence, and only minimal drool.

The man said Jackie had bipolar disorder

Octavia thought TMI!, but said, “Wait, I thought that was the fun one?”

The man looked at Octavia for a long while and then said after a deathly pall of silence had settled over his dank, airless apartment, “Fun some of the time, I suppose.”

“But then the other of the time, not so fun!” Octavia smiled.

The man had tears in his eyes, or maybe it was just the glaucoma. Octavia only got suspended for two weeks that time with reduced pay.

She was getting stronger.

Octavia's publisher repeated that she did not know if Florida had clothes.

"What does that mean?" Octavia tried to ask in a not screaming manner.

"I know about the cannibals," the publisher said, "but I imagine them as naked. The cannibals."

"I'm asking what type of clothes the average Floridian wears on an average Florida day," Octavia sighed. "Like do I bring a fucking North Face? Do I wear barbecue sandals - what?"

"It's like a big *swomp*," the publisher slurred. Octavia wondered if maybe the woman was not drunk or stroked but potentially a mentally handicapped. It would explain a lot. The Quiznos toaster position; being a "publisher". Every time Octavia got on the horn with the broad she was talking to her about jelly beans. Those gourmet kind that have like popcorn and poop flavor. She would have her bag of beans with her and be listing off the flavors as she ate them. Octavia would sit in stunned silence as the woman would pop a bean into her mouth, chew for a while, and then shout, "Root Beer!" or "Black Pudding!". What the fuck is black pudding.

Octavia, back in the bathroom, looked at Mary, who was looking at the Boston Market Baboon eating her entire chicken like it was a sandwich, and Octavia said, "What to wear in Florida?"

It had come out like a slur.

Mary turned to look at her, in her eyes she had the look that Octavia often had in her eyes when she saw a special person. One of those bicycle helmet drool types who waddled around like a baby but they have a grown person body so it's scary.

"What?" Mary had said without moving her mouth. She attempted cautious disgust. Octavia noticed she had a moustache and that it was styled and trimmed.

Octavia shook her head to be normal again, but then instantly regretted it, understanding at once it made her look even more incapacitated.

"I mean, what do you wear in Florida? I have a trip. I'm going to Florida soon and need to know what to-"

"Why are you asking me? Do I look like some sort of *expert* in Florida travel wear?" Mary demanded, offended.

"I mean you work at Macy's."

"Yeah, in the bathroom!" Mary shouted. She said bathroom weird again. Like bahfvruhm!

Octavia wanted to laugh but was scared so chose not to so the laugh reabsorbed back into her body and she knew later, she would have explosive diarrhea and maybe her colon would slough out, finally, and it'd all be done.

"Buy a fucking skort!" Mary shouted, "I don't know!"

"Ya get a flip flop and some gator jorts," the obese Boston Market said from her little area on the floor. She was gnawing away at her chicken carcass and she looked pleasantly plump and content.

Octavia took out her little notepad and scribbled some of the suggestions. She looked at Boston Marky.

"And now what is gator jorts."

"Ya get the jorts, and the gators can't tear 'em up."

Octavia started to put her notepad away. "I don't know what that means."

She looked back at Mary. "They don't teach you in training about what to wear, in all the different American sections?"

Mary looked hard at her. "You see me standing here in the fucking bahtfvhroom while bitches are up in here pissing and shitting with wild abandon and I gotta stand here and smile while my nose and mouth holes fillin' wit' piss and shit smells. You see that?" She looked deep at Octavia and though Octavia understood it was more of a rhetorical sort of question, she was also expected to genuinely answer.

Octavia nodded, "I see."

"So don't ask stupid questions." Then Mary went on, "And when I'm not here turning on the faucet for bitches after they just got finished shitting and instead of them using the faucet they speed right by with no type of soap or water touching those shitty little hands—When I'm not *here*, I'm selling houses. I have no education whatsoever concerning what they may or may not be adorning their bodies with in Florida. I've never been there. I'm still not sure it's a real place. I think it's just in a movie. I don't think it's a real place. I think it's like Kwanzaa. Some made up goofy shit to scare people!"

She was looking very hard and serious at Octavia. She had a booger kind of coming down her nose. Or maybe it was a glob of snot. All around her mouth and nose area looked like dried up snot. Her face looked like it hurt. Like it was very dry and itchy-looking and caked with mucus. Still, there was something vaguely glamorous or elegant about her. Maybe it was how she appeared to be Lord of the Bathroom. There was something impressive about that to Octavia and she wondered if it were a sexual thing. It usually was.

Eventually, Ock decided on, "You're a realtor?"

"What it look like?"

"It looks like you work in this bathroom in the basement at Macy's."

"Funny guy," Mary said with a dark, blank face; her eyes black and hard. "But guess what?" she said with hate in her chest. "I'm a realtor, *too*." It was like a verbal loogie hawk into the eye.

Octavia didn't know why, but she felt threatened and scared and like she'd been insulted. To combat this, she said, "Yeah, well, I wouldn't buy a house from you."

Mary said like it was nothing, "You don't have the money."

"I have plenty," Octavia countered.

"You look like you ride a fucking school bus part time and the other rest of the time you work in a prison cooking slop for rapists and murderers." Her mind wandered off for a spell, then she added, "For priests. For popes."

"I'm banned from the prison," was the best Octavia could come up with. "They wouldn't hire me on there, so look who looks fucking stupid?"

Mary was confident, unfazed. "Out of the two of us," she said, "Me the least."

"You work in a fucking bathroom," Octavia reminded Miss Thang.

"Hey!" the obese white said, her mouth full of carcass. She was pointing a big, greasy finger at Octavia.

Octavia looked at her. It was like as if a bear suddenly started talking.

The big white said, "Don't talk to my best fren like dat!"

Mary scoffed with disgust. "*Best friend?* I-"

"You know her?" Octavia asked, succulent with disgust. She was thinking about taking Mary off her Cool List for this.

"No!" Mary said, insulted. "This bitch killed her child. I aint being friends with a big bitch, an' especially no big bitch who killed her child."

Octavia was thinking about how she herself was big; would Mary not be friends with her. No, she probably just meant big whites. And in particular, big whites who killed their child.

"I ain' kill nobody," the big white drawled. "He dun fell down the mountain his'self."

"How a baby fall down a mountain, Big Debra?" Mary was saying and Octavia knew she had lied. Mary knew this woman. She knew all about her and how she threw her baby down a mountain.

"He fell his'self!" the woman reiterated. "How I'm s'posed to stop 'im?? You think I'm Superman?!"

"Superman would kill a child," Mary said with confidence. "He's an alien. He has zero connection to the human race. What's throwing a baby down a mountain to an alien? It's probably like squashing a fly to us."

The big white just stared.

Mary repeated that she wasn't being best friends with someone who killed their child.

"<u>Period</u>," she said, striking the air.

The big white started shaking her giant, sloppy ass head. "Yew judgemental. Das why u ain' got no bestfren. Only me."

“Only no one. Just me and me.” Mary folded her dark, dry arms across her chest and she looked proud and prideful.

Octavia didn’t know why, but she felt depressed. She felt real damp and gloomy. She felt like Mary would go home later that night and have some soup and in that soup would be a ton of laundry detergent. Octavia wondered if Mary even had a home. Could she afford detergent. She worked in a bathroom. Maybe she lived there, too.

“Hey, you should come with me to Florida,” Octavia was saying and before she was even done speaking Mary was saying, “I’d rather fucking kill myself.”

Octavia pressed on, saying, “Me and my homegirls are doing a big trip. So it won’t just be me there.”

“Homegirls,” Mary repeated with contempt.

“Can eye cum?” the big white said.

“No,” both Octavia and Mary answered quickly, with barely restrained contempt.

Octavia turned back to Mary, “So whaddya say?”. She had no idea whose voice that was that came out of her mouth. She wondered if she had a crush on Mary or what? She didn’t seem like a lesbian, she seemed barely human. She was very dry and her skin cracked. Ock’s usual type was ditzy lipstick chicks who know where the lotion aisle is located in the store.

Mary eyed Octavia up and down. At last, she answered with, “Is that a wooden arm?..”

“Yeah I got it ripped off during a fight when I was a kid.”

Mary turned up her lips like she was impressed.

“So whaddya say?” Octavia repeated. What am I doing? she wondered. Pretty much everything that happened to her was because of her doing some random shit that entirely confused her when she thought back to the moment. Like how she had a son. She’d decided to be hetero for like a week some time back and fuck a dude. Some random man she’d met at Garden Carcass Mall selling condoms outside of MetroPCS. Octavia walked up to him because she thought the condoms were free, that he was handing them out. Octavia didn’t use condoms because she was a lesbo and didn’t feel the need, but free was free. When she went up to Lamar, though, he demanded five dollars.

“Is that how much condoms cost?” Octavia said. No wonder a billion bitches having babies.

Lamar had turned to a man walking past and pointed, saying, “Look at him look at him! Why he walkin’ like dat? Look like he got shid in his ass.” He had turned to Octavia and said, “I look like that when I walk?”. He wasn’t really asking her because Octavia had never seen him walk. He said gazing off into the distance, “I wonder if I look like that when I walk.”

Octavia, trying to flirt, said, “I think that man is a homosexual.”

Lamar turned to her, “Okay, see, he got a dick still in his ass or some shit.”

His eyes said excited despite his voice expressing disgust.

So anyway Octavia let Lamar do a load into her. It was gross and she thought he had passed away during the act. In actuality, he had just blacked out because she used her butt plug on him and he passed out on top of her. Now she had a kid with the idiot. She’d thought about abortion but was too lazy to go down and get it sucked out so now she had a fucking kid. She just be doing shit. Or not doing shit, in the case of getting an abortion. Which she absolutely should’ve done. Octavian was cool and all but who the fuck is tryna take care of a kid, like, *forever?* Then she had to deal with Lamar's remedial ass. Still selling condoms. No one's buying them period, but especially not from out front of a MetroPCS. That's like tryna sell electric blankets in Hell. Come on now.

Mary said, "If we go to 'Florida'"--she did air quotes when she said Florida–"and we see an alligator, will you take your arm off and use it to club the gator in the head?"

"I don't know, I think I would be too shy to kill a gator," Octavia decided.

Mary thought for a moment. Then at last rejoined with, "Well, that would be the main draw for me, to attend this trip."

"Me clubbing a gator?"

Mary nodded. "But specifically, you ripping your wooden arm off to do the clubbing."

"Um, okay. I guess I'll think about it."

"Hmm.." Mary said, a touch disappointed. It was a bit too noncommittal for her liking.

"I still don't even know if this 'Florida' even exists," she decided after a while. "Maybe it'd be interesting to check out if it's an actual thing, like dinosaurs. Matter fact, I've never seen a gator, either. So this could be considered a little scientific excursion, if you will."

Octavia was the one to be like "Hmm" this time. Then, "So you'll go? My homegirls will love you," she lied.

Mary cringed at Octavia saying homegirls again.

She said, "Do I have to interact with them? Your…*homegirls*."

Octavia shrugged fatly, “Not if you don’t want to.”

Mary raised a brow, “And you’ll pay?”

Octavia wondered what Mary wondered was her specific motivation. Did she think Octavia was trying to recruit Mary as her sugar baby? Mary looked older. Octavia had never done the sugar baby thing on either side but she was pretty sure in order to be a sugar baby you have to be younger than the sugar mommy or daddy, or no?

“I’ll have to bring my first cousin, Yolanda,” Mary said, after Octavia did not answer the money question. It was clear that Mary had taken the silence as a yes.

“Yolanda?..” Octavia said, wondering why life insisted on carrying on.

“She’s my caretaker,” Mary said.

Oh god, Octavia thought.

“..Caretaker?”

“I need a…guardian. Because of my severe mental illness. The court said so.”

“Mmm..”

“But as long as Yolanda can come, and as long as she can bring her oxygen machine, it’s a go!”

Octavia just stared.

“Um,” she started.

Mary, without provocation, went on to explain that she'd been in prison for a decade or so - having been released only very recently.

"I was a home health aide. You know, spoonin' slop to retards and discarded elderly - things like that."

Octavia nodded to indicate she understood simple concepts. Octavia thought about her mother who had home health aides come to her apartment to rub diabetes lotion on her feet and legs because Octavia refused to do it because she didn't like the bitch. She was big and she'd been abusive. Whenever she got a new boyfriend she'd dump Octavia on her grandmother, who was even bigger and more of a bitch. Octavia swore she'd get her revenge on these beasts. Though when the time came, she did much of nothing. Her grandmother died unexpectedly while Octavia was still in college so she hadn't been there to dance and spit on her deathbed or whatever it was she'd planned to do. Octavia had never really lived long term with her mom and had never developed much of a relationship with her. She thought how it'd be more satisfying to have grown up consistently under the roof of her mother's, having been spat upon on a daily basis, so that when she is older and her mother is older and weaker, there could take place a sickening reversal of power dynamics. Octavia fantasized about it all happening under the same roof. She'd become an adult, become as big as her mother had been when she cowered over Octavia as a child, and then she would whoop her mother like her mother did her, but it'd be worse somehow, because Ock'd be whoopin' on some feeble old woman. Bones full of holes from all the hate coursing through her system. Her joints grinded down to dust from being a slut for decades.

Nic kind of had that scenario, but it was her dad instead of her mom and grandma. Nic's dad was a big bitch her entire childhood. When she became an adult, still living in his home, he was savagely beaten by the criminal organization he belonged to. Nic never spoke much about her dad's gangster business, but he was a gigantic asshole, a loud mouth, so it wasn't difficult to guess he'd pissed off some big boss and now he was loaded with lumps and knots and his head was partially off. He was beaten terribly; disfigured. Now he expected Nic to take care of him, but instead, she just left him to rot. His body was found a few weeks later, decaying and covered with maggots and flies, by his landlord. Nic was brought up on charges for second degree manslaughter or neglect of an invalid or some such malarky, but she ended up only getting like a year probation and she was required to attend family counseling which she thought was hilarious because her family was all deceased, gone. In the end, she won.

Octavia wished for a satisfying scenario like that, but her reality was that her mother had taken ill, so Ock called up Medicaid to get her a home health aide and they looked after her. Ock's older sister was married and had her own picture-perfect family now. To look like a good daughter to people on Facebook, she dropped by occasionally on their mom to clean and to cook. She'd post photos of their mother in her little hospital bed they had set up in the living room, with her sparse hairs freshly combed, a strained smile upon her face. She told Ock she barely even acknowledged the woman when she visited. Never spoke to her (she never said a word when she took the photos, or explained what she was doing) or asked what groceries she wanted - it was all for show. They knew their mom wouldn't complain on Facebook to relatives. She only posted adoring posts about them and her grandkids - acting like all was well. In a way, that was a kind of satisfying "ending" to the cycle, Octavia thought, though there was still time for her abandoned corpse to be discovered by neighbors like three weeks after she's dead because of the stench of her decomposing body. There was still time for that, Octavia thought with a smile.

"What about that is inspiring a smile from you?" Mary was demanding, causing Octavia to come-to.

"I tell you I poisoned my client's soup and refused to change his diaper and you think it's cute?"

Octavia looked at her. There was something sexy about Mary's criminal record. She was dangerous, a rebel.

"They told me I'm a manic bipolar," Mary went on, scoffing. She looked intensely at Octavia, "I'm the sanest motherfucker you will *ever* know."

She looked off for a moment, pondering on something. Octavia felt an excitement, a rush of fear. It was one of those moments where you're pretty sure this is it, your death. Octavia thought how it seemed most humans, all infallible, all vulnerable to death, all who will suffer from the end of life–She thought how the lot of them didn't worry about when that time would exactly come, what it would be like. Octavia herself rarely thought about death. Not even during her suicidal middle school days. The darkest days of her life. When she loved that fifty year old homosexual Korean man - there was no reason for her to live then, and yet, she never really considered when it would all be over, and how. It was more of an abstract notion, like oxygen. Just some random unseen phantom hovering around at all times, but never an entirely real, graspable concept. Or, at least not to someone like Octavia, who thought just because you're a lesbian you were impervious to STDs.

Octavia came back to Mary saying, "Implying I tried to kill that old man because I have a mental illness is insulting. I am always lucid. I am in my right mind, always. I knew exactly what I was doing. No invisible hand guided me. I tried to kill him because I didn't like him. It's simple."

Octavia nodded and it was in genuine agreement. She understood completely. The old man had probably been a big bitch his entire life, and Mary could sense it. Maybe he even exposed his whole self to her, his real self. She'd seen his forked tongue and decided he should be removed. That being said...Octavia, despite only knowing Mary for a few minutes, she would not consider her a mentally sane individual. She would consider her the least mentally stable person she has ever come across. And one time she came across a Mexican lawyer wearing cowboy boots and jeans, on his way to a murder trial. Octavia had sat next to him on the bus. She'd asked him if his lawyer job didn't pay enough money for him to have a car. He said he had a horse. Come to think of it, Octavia thought, maybe that man wasn't a lawyer, after all...

Octavia heard herself saying, “I know what you mean. I do meals-on-wheels and I have to deliver like plates of mashed potatoes and cranberry sauce to invalids and I hate the look of all of them. I think I’m jealous. They just sit in their little rooms and wait for me to send them free plates of food. Though, granted, the food is slop. Dogshit. Like, literally sometimes just shit they scrape off the grease trap from the local homeless shelter. They only really get good stuff on holidays like Thanksgiving and Kwanzaa.”

“Kwanzaa isn’t a thing or a holiday.”

Octavia nodded in agreement and carried on. “And like, even on Thanksgiving, the slop is the same, just they put a scoop of stuffing on the plate and the cranberry sauce is real instead of jelly.”

“I don’t know what most of those words mean put together,” Mary was saying, looking hard at Octavia. She squinted, then said, “What is meals-on-wheels? Is it you riding around on a bicycle chucking plates of mashed potatoes into people’s windows like I imagine?”

“More or less,” Octavia said, and though she couldn’t see herself from Mary’s perspective, she knew she looked and sounded super cool in that moment.

Mary had a look of grim, cemented discomfort on her face. She scanned Octavia up and down, in what Octavia felt like was an attempt on her part to discern Octavia’s exact species.

To reroute the situation, Octavia clarified, “I’m not on a bike. I don’t know how to ride a bike. I ride a bus. Sometimes I chuck the meal, depending on if it's accessible to do so, but a lot of time I have to go inside to deliver the meals, which really eats into my lunch break.”

Mary said eventually, “So I was right about the bus?”

Octavia started to speak but Mary said, “But you see I’m not crazy?”

“Well, I can’t speak to that. But I know, from doing meals-on-wheels, and shuttling a bunch of bad ass Bebe’s kids around on the school bus all day, that attempted murder isn’t like, *off-top* the most insane thing you could consider or put into action. It’s a natural response, I think, to fools, and to general society.”

“And to old people,” Mary added. “I don’t like them.”

Octavia thought Mary’s reasoning for wishing to commit murder almost definitely fell under the Mentally Insane Reasons 2 Kill category. It was one thing to want to kill someone for being a douche or an idiot, but wanting to kill simply because a person was old? Mary was old herself. Or maybe she was just African.

But Octavia was already invested in Mary. They were to be friends. Octavia never knew why she was interested in anyone. She never thought about it. Best not to think about it. So, she said, to make it like she agreed, “I don’t like olds, either. My grandma was old and she’s dead now.”

Mary nodded approval. “Good,” she said.

Octavia felt complete somehow, from this validation.

So it was decided that Mary would come on the Florida trip, and she’d be bringing her first cousin and guardian, Yolanda.

Yolanda had been appointed Mary’s conservator, after she was released from prison early for good behavior. Mary said, really, she’d been released because she had fought every Big Boss in the pen, and hadn’t died. “I never got raped,” she’d said proudly. She claimed she had gotten Too Big, too powerful for the prison. She had risen like a phoenix from every obstacle thrown her way. Octavia thought the sentence Mary had been given, and the time she served, seemed fairly reasonable. Ten years was a long time. Mary's story about beating all the big bosses and being too intimidating to the prison staff sounded like pure fantasy, but Octavia had never been in prison. She'd only seen it on TV. She could definitely believe Mary hadn't been raped, as she seemed more like the raper. If anything, Mary had probably been released from priz for adapting too well. That's not what *they* want, probably.

"Yolanda never has a man," Mary had offered as a small disclaimer concerning her cousin. "So she's like, desperate."

Octavia didn't know what Mary was trying to tell her. It sounded like a warning?

"Okay?" she said, and Mary grimaced with disgust, and parroted *"Okay?"* in a voice that made Octavia wonder if that was how she spoke. She felt sick.

"Okay," Mary went on. "So this woman, this *person*, if you want to call her that, is in a bad way. She's not like you"--and when she said this Mary looked at Octavia with so much disgust in her eyes it was like they were oozing pus with disgust–"she don't know about Bush World. So she waitin' around for some magical negro to come and quench her thirst, if you know what I mean."

Octavia didn't want to seem uncool, but she had to respond with, "No, not really…" she felt so dumb.

Mary sucked her teeth with annoyance. "She's *susceptible*, is what I'm telling you."

Octavia started to get a handle on what she was trying to get across.

Octavia had her long, LesbianPlus wallet out. She used it to scratch at the exposed scalp between her locs.

"Um, okay. So…you don't want your cousin to lick puss?" she said at last, to which Mary dramatically grimaced in pain.

"Yuck!" she said, sticking out her tongue. She shook her head like she was trying to eradicate a sickness that had gotten inside of her.

"Blech!" she carried on.

Octavia flattened her eyes at the display.

She said, "Why do you care if your cousin wants to…visit Bush World?"

Mary stuck her hand out right into Octavia's face, her palm almost touching Octavia's nose. Her hand smelled like brown sugar maple oatmeal, and gasoline.

"Pause!" Mary screamed.

Octavia closed her eyes to the hand and the smell.

She could feel Mary retract her hand and reopened her eyes to Mary staring at her with crazed, reddened eyeballs. "Just keep your paws off my cousin. She's *slow*. She'll be easy prey for you to do things to. She won't be able to fight you off. She won't know to."

Octavia was offended. "I'm not going to do anything to your cousin?" Then Octavia thought about it for a moment and said, "Wait, is she cute?"

Mary made a sound of disgust, then pulled up her Boost Mobile to show Octavia a photo. Yolanda looked like Luther Vandross with a long, silky sidebang. Octavia wasn't *not* into it.

"So, there!" Mary had said, putting away her phone.

On the way to the food court to see if they had Boston Market, Octavia had time to wonder what Mary had meant by that. So there? So there, what?

"All The Things She Said" by t.A.T.u. was playing ominously overhead as Octavia walked through the mostly empty mall. She spotted the MetroPCS kiosk where she had met her baby daddy and she cringed.

What would Mary think? Octavia wondered. Mary would definitely have some smart ass, totally unhinged shit to say about Octavia being a baby momma. Octavia considered not taking Octavian on the trip. Then she thought that was probably Bad Mom 101 to try and hide your child from a potential new friend so they don't drag you for getting cummed in and being too lazy to get an abortion.

Octavia cringed just thinking about Mary's response once she found out.

At the food court, praise Jehovah, there was Boston Market. Octavia almost cried when she saw it.

When she walked up to the counter, however, there was disappointment.

There was Phil.

"We're closed, ma'am," his ashy butt said. His lips dry like cereal.

"..Philliam?" Octavia said, and she was sick.

Phil didn't have his glasses on, so he squinted in Octavia's blurry direction. He then reached to the glasses hanging around his neck by a lanyard and pulled them on to his face. Still squinting, but with more clarity, his eyes widened. They looked like a creature's eyes from behind the frame.

"Octavia! Long time no see!"

Octavia wanted to throw up. She couldn't stand Phil. He smelled like boogers and you could not see his hairline if you were shorter than him and standing face to face. Octavia was a few inches shorter, so from her vantage point, he looked like he was in the radiation booth getting leukemia treatments. Octavia thought how she wouldn't eat food from him.

"Oh, okay, well," Octavia said, and she moved to turn away.

"Ock ock ock!" he cried, begging for her return. She froze in place, stuck, sickened.

Octavia moved back to the counter and stared.

"Wait a minute, Octavia," Phil said at Octavia standing there, waiting.

He went into the back part of Boston Market and returned with a bundled newspaper. He handed it over the counter to Octavia.

"Not sure if Amander gave you a copy," he said proudly, with feigned shyness.

Octavia looked down at the paper. *Senior Citizen Gazette*. The paper Phil did his soup reviews for. The paper that published his far the fuck back hairline inspired poems and haikus.

Octavia wanted to say, Why would Amander give me a copy of this? But instead she forced a tight smile and said fakely, "Wow!"

She thought to add some extra comment, but she was familiar enough with Phil to know she didn't need to. Instantly she could see joyful tears spring to his eyes. Her wow indicated to Phil that he'd only remain an employee at Boston Market but for a moment. He was destined for greater things than standing in a closed restaurant in a dilapidated mall that's foot traffic is like fifty people a year.

“Thanks for this,” Octavia said in the same fake voice, and she gestured the paper at Phil. She already had it rolled up in her hand like she was going to beat a dog. She quickly went to tuck the paper into the back pocket of her GirlPlus MissBig-sized FUBU jeans, saying what she hoped would complete the interaction, “Can’t wait to dig into this.”

“Actually,” Phil started, and something hard dropped down into Octavia’s stomach and ass.

Phil said none of his other coworkers had shown up to work for the day. He made it sound like it was a ton of people who hadn’t shown up but only him and another guy named Lionelle had been scheduled. Phil said he texted Lionelle to see if he would be coming in and received a text back from someone claiming to be Lionelle’s mother saying he’d been shot in the head at Six Flags and wouldn’t be making it into work today.

“I’m pretty sure it was just Lionelle making up some excuse,” Phil had said with a sigh. “He probably stayed at home to have sex. He lives with his mom but she lets him have his girlfriend stay overnight sometimes. His girlfriend is Hispanic. He’s always telling me about it. How she’s Hispanic and eats beans with everything. But if it were a British girlfriend would he brag the same?”

Octavia discovered Lionelle was sixteen, and had a dent in his head from being dropped hard on a cement floor as a baby by his mom’s boyfriend at the time.

“So now she’s always trying to compensate for that by letting him do whatever he wants, you know, out of guilt,” Phil, a forty-eight year old man, was saying with jealousy in his voice about a child.

And this was all before they had sat down to eat.

It was Phil’s idea. He said there were two more meals, conveniently leftover from earlier in the day, and that they could take and eat them. They were not warm, but Phil said they could go down to the Chinese restaurant and use their microwave.

When they went down to the Chinese restaurant to use their microwave the Chinese woman whom Phil spoke to said she did not want any "baboons" in her shop. Octavia felt bad so pretended to be a cop. She took out the fake security badge she uses to intimidate her meals-on-wheels clients into letting her take items from their homes. And then they were able to use the microwave.

Octavia wasn't in the position of being able to turn down spending time with Phil. Everyone in the "crew" had to at the very least, engage with him if he initiated contact or conversation. Amander didn't play about her ugly man, or her son. She would do something to hurt (bodily or otherwise) you if you disrespected them. So you couldn't talk about Phil's hairline, or how their son Franklin had a fifty-four year old girlfriend that was also one of Amander's coworkers. You had to just nod and smile.

The girls had all gotten together semi-recently, apart from Amander of course, to discuss possibly extracting her from the group.

"Is she even pertinent?" Barb had posited.

"I always think about her taking semen from Phil to make Franklin and it makes me have a low opinion of her," was babymama Philly's contribution.

"She's a serial killer, for sure," Nic had speculated, to which Leece responded, "You have HIV." But what Nic said had set them all straight. Because, it was more than possible. The idea–No, the *reality* of this, was very much on the table. So they tabled the get rid of Amander discussion.

Octavia herself liked Amander. She didn't know why and never thought about it. It was just Phil she couldn't take. Why couldn't he go away or die? People die every day. It was always the ones you couldn't stand who insisted on persisting.

Phil brought out two tablets of Boston Market meals. They were in these little black plastic trays. They were dissimilar to the trays Octavia handed out for meals-on-wheels, which were white styrofoam trays that only had three sections. One section for the meat, one for veg slop or cranberry slop, and one for mashed potatoes, or corn, or french fries, depending on the time of year. Mashed potato from November into February. Fries from March until July 4th and then it's corn until Halloween.

Removing the plastic cover to her tray revealed a slab of what was probably chicken, though it could have been a turkey or pork cutlet. Octavia studied it and felt seventy-eight percent confident that it was chicken, though she wasn't particular about her meat. Despite being a lesbian, she would accept into her mouth any form or matter of meat. Even chuck. She ate whatever. As long as it gave off a meatly presence, she'd eat it.

Next to the boiled, unseasoned slab of meat was a glob of cranberry sauce. Octavia turned up her nose. She didn't like cranberry sauce and she didn't like that it was touching the meat.

Under the meat, disgustingly, was a soggy bed of string beans. In a section adjacent to the beans sat a confounding lump of white. Mashed potatoes, perhaps. Octavia felt like she was on her death bed being ignored by hateful, demented nurses. They leave this boiled, unseasoned slop sitting out on her dinner tray even though they know she is incapacitated and has a tube. Maybe they leave the "meal" to taunt her. Octavia doesn't know in which manner they wish her to suffer. Is she supposed to be grieving for when she used to be able to take solids? Or is she meant to be upset thinking about the fact that if she were capable of eating, it could only be the grey, digested-looking food they steamed in the hospital kitchen cauldron? Octavia didn't know. In her little fantasy she is in a white hospital room that has visible scum on the walls, and the blanket on her bed is brown. She has no relatives come visit her. Possibly they do not know she is even in the hospital (a Jane Doe scenario), or if they know, they don't care.

While Octavia was spiraling down the rabbit hole, Phil was saying things from his mouth.

Octavia caught up with Phil saying something about parchment.

God, she thought.

"She had moved my parchment," Phil was saying, wide-eyed behind his greasy glasses. He was shaking his head and some lint stuffs and dandruff was coming off. "I can't write without my parchment."

Octavia looked up from the slab of chicken she had been vainly poking at with her plastic spork.

"Mmm," she said to Phil's expectant face. He smiled solely off her responding to him.

Then he kept staring, so Octavia knew the "mmm" wasn't actually as satisfactory as his warm smile had made it seem, and she was unreasonably angry, but concealed it with a cool mask that she used to say, "I didn't know you worked at Boston Market. Amander didn't say. Last thing I heard you were involved in was some sort of medical trial?"

Octavia knew the medical trial had gone awry and Phil had suffered an injury and was currently embroiled in a lawsuit suing the medical company for damages. She was just being messy for asking. Trying to exorcise her hatred for him through a manner in which she felt was better than just bashing his head in with a giant rock. She didn't see a rock around, so this was the next best thing.

A darkness cast itself across Phil's visage just then, and then suddenly he was flopping up from his seat. "Hyung!" he went, as he hauled his body from the dilapidated food court chair. It was a weird chair of olive green ceramic that was a clear castover from the nineties, the last time the Garden Carcass Mall had undergone a remodel.

Phil flopped across the food court, without a word, to the Auntie Anne's, and Octavia watched him walk up to the counter as if he had to wait in line, but no one was standing there. From the back of him, he appeared to be standing patiently as if it were. Octavia watched as one of the Auntie Anne's employees moved to take Phil's order with dead-eyed disinterest.

They wish him dead as well as me, Octavia thought in a voice not unlike her own.

After a while, Phil was flopping back over to Octavia with his wares.

He slopped a bag onto the inappropriately-gleaming salmon-colored table. He reached into the bag and retrieved a cinnamon sugar coated pretzel and handed it over to Octavia.

"For you, mi'lady."

My god, Octavia thought, in shock.

She wondered, Is Phil tryna fuck?

He knew Octavia was a puss master. Well, maybe not a master, but definitely a purveyor. And he knew the only dick she ever took was Lamar's, during a rare manic episode. And it was just the one time because Octavia wasn't really one of those mentally ill type of broads. She didn't really have the countenance to be unhinged. She didn't have the energy or interest. The weirdest shit she was capable of was writing *As Told By Ginger* erotic fanfiction. That was as mentally ill as it got for Octavia. She wasn't in the mood for all that extra bipolar or depression or schizophrenic shit. She'd leave that to the bitches who worked at or managed a Forever 21. It was not her portion.

Octavia watched as Phil sank back into his seat, making all sorts of "hyung" noises. She hadn't noticed that about him before: the noises. Was it something new? Admittedly, she tried very hard anytime she was forced to be around Phil, to not pay attention to him. She always tried to fulfill her bare minimum ~acknowledge Phil~ duties to satisfy Amander. For Octavia that was vaguely glancing in his direction and saying either "hi" or "bye". And that was usually enough. This Boston Market thing was unusual for them. It was a unique situation, and Octavia was sweating and afraid. She was sure she would snap and break his head off. How long would this last, she worried. She didn't have long, she felt.

"Hyung!" Phil did, and something moved in his neck.

Octavia could not contain her fear or disgust and displayed it openly. Phil acknowledged it with a somber nod.

"The ManBeast Scheinfeld-JiJermaine-KKKlaxon trials."

What are those words? Octavia thought. Why is his neck like that? Why does his hairline start all the way at the back of his head?

"The ManBeast tablets," Phil continued on, to clarify. He took a bite of his Cool Ranch Doritos dust and Herbs de Provence coated pretzel.

Octavia ogled Phil's hand. Well, it was a claw, really. His nails were long and thick in an unnatural way and curved under like a creature's.

Phil acknowledged her gaping and nodded again, saying again, "It's the ManBeast tablets…". He sighed with sadness. Octavia thought he should be captured and put down.

"What are ManBeast tablets?" she asked with fear and disgust.

Phil sighed with melancholy. "It was what was given to me at the Scheinfeld-JiJermaine-KKKlaxon laboratory. Didn't Amander tell you?"

“She doesn’t talk about you to me,” Octavia said quickly. She didn’t think about what she was saying, or how it sounded. In truth, Amander, thankfully, did not discuss her family much with the crew. It was a blessing. She was very, like, *into* her husband and son. She was constantly with them and doing shit with them and all sorts of questionable nonsense. Neither Phil nor Franklin were okay, human-wise. It wasn’t okay to like, be super into either of them. Franklin played violin, for god’s sake. And Phil was, well, a creature. Even before the ManBeast trials, so what was Amander’s excuse?

Phil, unfazed by Octavia’s comment, carried on talking and it was the worst.

He clacked his browned talons together, studying them. “They really made a mess of me,” he laughed. He looked at Octavia, “But they were paying eight hundred dollars. You take a mysterious pill for three months and at the end of the three months you get eight hundred dollars put on a Visa or Amazon gift card.”

He was saying this with wonder and amazement displayed upon his face.

“Do you know how many soup reviews I have to write to make eight hundred dollars? How many *poems* I have to churn out? Like, *millions*. For poems, anyway. For soup reviews I’d have to churn out eight hundred soup reviews. *In three months?*” He pondered in a dramatic fashion. “It’s possible, writing-wise. But I don’t even think eight hundred soups exist.” He looked intensely at Octavia, *“Do you?”*

Octavia said she knew clam chowder and bean.

“What is bean soup?..” Phil asked as if the entire world had suddenly gaped open upon his feet.

Octavia said, “Exactly what it sounds like. Soup with bean, baby.” She didn’t know why she responded to him like that. Also, she knew other soups. Chicken Noodle and Italian Wedding. But she remembered them too late, plus she wasn't sure Italian Wedding was a real soup or maybe she had just dreamed it and it wasn't an actual thing. You had to be careful mentioning shit from dreamworld like it was an actual thing. That's how you get sent to crazytown.

"So that's two soups," Phil said, laughing. "Two dollars. It'd take me three months just to think of eight hundred soups. You see why I signed up for the medical trial? Way easier money. But nothing's worth it if you don't work for it, right?"

Octavia didn't agree. She wasn't about to work hard. And if a gajillion dollars fell into her lap right that minute without her having to lift a finger, well, she'd be dead. Splattered to death, because that's a lot of money. It'd be heavy and all of her organs would be crushed into a fine dust.

But to Phil, she nodded, "Yup. That's what my granny always says."

Her granny never said such a thing. She never called her grandmother "granny" ever in her life. Her grandmother is dead from complications due to AIDS.

"Well," Phil said, nodding, "your granny is right."

She was never right, Octavia thought. She was a dumb bitch, and it took far too long for Satan to reach up from the bowels of Hell and yank her back home.

"I tried to get fast money," Phil said, his head down. Finally, Octavia could see the hairline. It was in a U-shape at the top of his dome. His exposed scalp wasn't shiny, but crispy and covered in scales. "Tried to do things the easy way. The faster you get it, the quicker it leaves you, right?"

Octavia didn't know if she agreed. She thought things worked more randomly than that. She didn't believe in any sort of set universe rules. She didn't believe in gravity.

"Did you get the eight hundred dollars?" Octavia heard herself saying.

Phil sighed. "I had to give up a few weeks into it because of suffering a bad reaction to the medication. Or, the medication worked, but I couldn't handle the side effects. Or the intended effects, whatever you want to call it."

"Oh, right," Octavia said in a bored voice. Her life force was draining and she was losing herself to the abyss. "I think Amander mentioned you were doing a lawsuit?"

Phil sighed with ash. "The lawyer is saying it might not be possible because I accepted a fifteen dollar Brookstone gift card as compensation for the time I spent on the trial."

"You have a lawyer?" Octavia was impressed. She didn't think Phil had a bank account.

"Yeah, Mexican chap. Wears cowboy boots. Cowboy hat. I thought he looked like he could really make something happen."

"Hmm," Octavia said, her face deadened and slack.

"Hyung!" Phil moaned from his body. He was having like some little seizure in his chair? Octavia just stared.

Some homeless woman shuffled by, dragging her bag of trash. She walked over while Phil was convulsing and tapped him on the hunch of his back.

Phil's eyes shot up to the woman. She smelled like Quiznos.

"Excuse me, good gentleman," she said in a fancy voice. Phil fought to tamp down his convulsing so he could accommodate the woman.

"By chance, are you African American?"

"Yes?" Phil nodded, as if she asked him if he was Denzel Washington or something.

The homeless woman started to talk, some sort of poll she was taking having to do with rates of unemployment among black men, despite the fact that she was dragging around a bag of trash that a bit of someone's human leg was sticking out of and also her coat was one of those big ugly puffy coats that always have feather coming out of them and you could see she had patches of duct tape over all the little holes to try to keep the feathers in and Octavia wondered how she afforded the duct tape. Duct tape was as expensive as the coat. Maybe she stole the tape. She should steal a new coat, Octavia thought. And maybe steal some Febreze and Listerine, cuz…

"Aren't you from Canada?" Octavia interjected.

Phil looked at her. "Nova Scotia, born and bred," he smiled.

What the fuck, Octavia thought, disturbed. "So how are you african-ameri "

"I'm of African origin, and I live in America, so *yes*." he smiled psychotically. The homeless woman had already shuffled on. Phil noticed and jerked his head back, disappointed at her exiting.

"She didn't finish her questioning of me…" he said despondently.

Octavia was offended he seemed to desire the company of that trash bag woman more than her. Sure, Octavia hated his guts and wished for his death every second, but what the fuck.

“I have a question,” she said, shaking. Then suddenly she was calm and no longer cared, but she had already started the prompt and had to carry it through. She gestured over to the darkened Boston Market. And that was her question.

Phil explained that he got the job at Boston Market at first just to distract himself from the disappointment of the failed ManBeast medical trials. Then, he quickly became inspired and got an idea for something new to work on. He said he was working at Boston Market now for “research”.

“I’m working on a new project,” he smiled, and his teeth were small like a baby’s. “A novel.” He looked with intense desire into Octavia’s face. “Like you.”

“Like me, what?” Octavia was afraid.

“I’m writing a book like how you write books. Except mine won’t be sexy. Or, that’s not the plan, anyway. It’s about soup.”

Octavia raised her eyebrows. “You’re writing a book about *soup?* Like a recipe book..?”

Phil shook his head and some bits fell off. Octavia couldn’t see if it was chunks of skin or bits of his aura chipping away or… “It’s about an elderly man who has a goal of eating all the soups he can muster until he dies.”

What the fuck, Octavia thought, but said from her mouth, instead, “That sounds erotic to me.”

Phil blushed and looked diseased. “Ah, well…” and he was sweating. “That’s not the plan…”

Octavia started to feel interested in Phil, for the first time. He can’t be a real person, she thought. She observed him, considered his form, and reminded herself well, he was Canadian, it was not likely at all that he was human, at least not all the way.

“Well, you know what they say,” Octavia chuckled in a false tone, “When we plan, God…” Octavia had to stop playing games and actually seriously think about what the quote was. Was it a quote? God probably didn’t have any famous quotes, right? It was like Santa Claus or something, maybe? Did she look foolish quoting this man? This imaginary fat white man? She looked insane, she realized, but then Phil made it less cringe on her end by going,

“Oh, no, I don’t believe in God. I’m a Satanist.”

“Alright,” Octavia said and for some reason her stomach started to bubble. Phil being a demon would make the most sense. He had no hairline and was from Canada. That would explain basically all of it.

“I mean,” Phil choked on a bit of his pretzel. He paused to hack and spew some chunks to Octavia’s side of the table, and from where she was sitting, she had to sit and be still and calm. She couldn’t react in disgust to him spewing chewed-up bits of pretzel basically almost on to her person. She had to just sit and look on. She thought maybe she should walk over and pound on his back; make it look like she was helping, but before she could get into gear, Phil was fine and breathing mostly normal. There was a slight rattly-wheeze, but that had been there before.

“I mean,” he continued. “I believe in God” (he said “God” like “Gawd”), “it’s just I won’t listen to him.”

“Fine by me,” Octavia said, and her stomach was really bubbling over. It was getting closer to her ass and soon there’d be an emergency.

“I still celebrate Kwanzaa, though.”

“Kwanzaa isn’t a thing, it’s not a real thing,” Octavia was saying as she began to stand up from the table, gripping the upper part of her pussy area. It mostly just looked like she was holding up her GirlPlus MissBig-sized FUBU jeans, though they were on pretty snug.

“Look, Phil, I’ve gotta jet.” Octavia had never said “I’ve gotta jet” ever before in her life. She thought maybe some part of her subconscious was attempting to get through to Phil, find a soul in there somewhere, but Octavia wished her subconscious would stop wasting time with that and get busy fixing itself so Octavia could be normal and stop having to go to bed in her winter coat because that’s the only way she can get to sleep.

Phil looked seriously at Octavia. “Kwanzaa is very real, Octavia. As real as Brazilian jiu jitsu fighting. As real as the Macarena.”

Octavia was pretty sure–not entirely but pretty–that all those things Phil listed were made-up things from movies. But she didn’t have the time, or interest, to be going back and forth with him. She’d acknowledged him, and then gone beyond her typical call of duty to fucking sit and have a meal and be forced to watch him chew on his food like some sort of squirrel, alternating between nibbling on his wares, and storing chunks in his cheeks. Octavia had done more than required by sitting there and pretending everything was fine and normal instead of getting up and roundhouse kicking his crispy little head off.

Phil sat his dusty self back in his seat, and watched as Octavia hustled and bustled herself up and away from the table. He studied her for a moment before speaking.

After a while, he asked, “Well, where are you off to, Octavia? We’ve just sat down to lunch.”

Octavia looked at him, sweat collecting on her brow. She had strategic cuts in her brow to indicate to the other scissor sisters that she was one of them. Philly had said the eyebrow cuts weren’t necessary. According to her,

Octavia was “a stud muffin with Stevie Wonder locs - they know, girl”. Octavia had thought part of that was a compliment, but then Philly had clarified that by “stud muffin” she meant “big and brolic with a muffin-shaped torso”. Octavia decided that Philly was jealous that she only liked men and couldn’t be in the cLub. She had like seventy baby daddies and had never once been asked to be a character on some ratchet reality show. She did all that silly hetero shit - and for what? She was just jealous. And she would look stupid if she had locs (jaundiced-tone), and even stupider if she was a lesbian. Octavia couldn’t imagine Philly trying to eat pussy. She’d do something weird like sniff it first before licking it with just the tippy top of her tongue a few times in utter repulsion and then start getting tears in her eyes, and *not* the helpful kind. Not the sexy kind.

“I’ve gotta get jeans cream for the trip,” Octavia said, really sweating. It wasn’t just droplets, but pouring from her holes. She was really about to mess up the Garden Carcass Mall bathroom. She wanted to go back to the one in Macy’s, but she was afraid of running into Mary again, in this post-having-to-acknowledge-Phil state she was in. The next time she saw Mary she wanted to be fresh. She didn’t want to be looking like she had just went to town on a bunch of expired Brisk peach iced teas from Quiznos. She didn’t want to look like she was actively fighting off botulism.

Phil looked interested, and alone. He said, to keep her there, “What is jeans cream?”

“Cream for your jeans!” Octavia shouted as she hustled away from holding the bottom of her butt closed with her LesbianPlus wallet. She’d have to text an apology to Amander later (she didn’t have Phil’s number and didn’t want to have it), explaining why she had cut out of lunch with Phil so early. Octavia wasn’t too worried about it. Amander probably liked her the most out of everyone in the crew. It was between her and Barb, and Amander only “liked” Barb because she was afraid of Barb. Barb was older, she had been alive when the Grey Butt Bus was just a bicycle with a little basket in the front. She’d *seen shit*.

Amander thought all the rest of the crew were silly sluts. It'd be worse if one of the other girls except for Barb had cut out early on Phil. It would be scarier. But Octavia wasn't concerned, though she knew there'd be some sort of consequence. She'd have to "make up" for it. She just hoped Amander wouldn't ask Ock to be a part of a threesome with them. She had always vaguely hinted about that, and Octavia always tried to vaguely hint that when she gets horny she gets very itchy and starts to shake. But that was a risk, because you never know, she could be into that. So far, it seemed, Amander wasn't. But there was still time. Octavia's taste in disgusting sexual shit changed all the time. Just a few weeks ago, and for months before that, she'd been deeply obsessed with any woman who looked like a Puerto Rican Princess Diana. The darker and thicker the accent the better. They had to have the hair, but the ass had to be phat. It was a very specific sort of desire and she was mad over it, entirely focused on just this one thing and then one day, all of a sudden, she was into Ninja Turtle bitches. The Puerto Rican beak-nosed princesses were out. It was like she had never been into that at all. So Octavia knew things could switch up at any moment. She just hoped and prayed Amander would never be into itchy, convulsing type of broads, though…she did have Phil in her bedroom. Octavia made a mental note to start implying she had something else sexually wrong with her around Amander to keep her off the threesome idea. *Kinky bush hair coming out of the butt,* she added to her notes.

Octavia sat on the toilet in the Garden Carcass Mall Food Court Bathroom For Handicaps Only!!! and pulled out her phone. She had a long phone, as long as her LesbianPlus wallet. Philly was always saying Octavia's long phone and long wallet and long face whenever Philly talked to her represented Octavia's deep-seated desire for long schlong.

"I already had Lamar," Octavia reminded Philly with disgust, cringing at her past self.

"Was he *long?*" Philly asked, too eager.

Octavia was sick to even hear the question, and then to think about it. She didn't know. What was long, *god, why me??*

Octavia pulled up a message thread between her and Ray, a mom she knew from Octavian's school, and a woman whom she sometimes did sex with. Ray was one of those ~of the earth~ hippie thots who had a million baby daddies like Philly, though she carried herself like it was all good (she wore a goddess chain to do the laundry), while Philly carried herself like the embarrassment she was (let her ugly daughter run the household).

Ray was skinny with huge knockers and always wearing crop tops to PTA meetings. All the other PTA moms stayed talking shit about her. She'd famously fucked the very married Principal of the school and when the kid they made started going to the school he had to quit and become a crossing guard. The only ones who didn't despise Ray was Octavia, because Octavia wanted to smash, and a much older mom, Jill, who didn't seem especially interested in Ray one way or the other. Jill was very involved with canning and preserving strawberries and blueberries and things she grew in a little garden at her house. She had a trans husband called Gary who worked crossing guard duty with the former Principal and was more liked by the kids than all the other crossing guards, even though he was always wearing this old, grey, misshapen wig that looked like he'd picked it up out of the sewers. And he wore sandals and was named Gary. Before Ray came, everyone hated Jill the most.

Octavia sat on the Garden Carcass Mall handicap toilet, pooping. She looked at her phone. In the beginning, when she'd first arrived to the bathroom, she could do nothing but groan and try not to die. It was a hurty one for a while there, but then the worst of it passed and she was able to sit more calmly on the bowl, without clenching in great agony, sweating blood like before.

She was able to breathe evenly and her vision could focus. She had wanted to reread the convo she'd had with Ray about the jeans cream.

Octavia had mildly discussed her Florida plans with Ray, and Ray, who figured herself a traveling-to-Florida expert ("I go to Miami like every other month with my girls") (sometimes she called her girls her "squad" in all seriousness), had recommended a product she deemed a "lifesaver": jeans cream.

"You will not regret this purchase," Ray had pitched like a salesman.

Octavia had texted, *"...U go 2 Miami every other month? That's deranged..."*

Ray responded with the crying-laughing emoji, but nothing was fucking funny. Nothing at all.

Octavia had wanted to call back to the convo to see where it was you bought the cream. Really, she had wanted to look over the conversation again and recall what exactly it was the jeans cream...*did*. What were its qualities or properties - anything. You couldn't necessarily discern it's purpose purely off the name. Though it was a simple name, it left much open to interpretation, and Octavia preferred the utmost clarity. She wasn't one for guesstimating. She had tried to look up "jeans cream" online, but there were little results. She had found, on Etsy, that someone was making jean-coverings for bottles of lotion and diaper rash cream. Octavia had no idea why anyone would do or want that, but it did not seem to be the product Ray had raved to her about. Though looking over the convo, Ray *had* provided info on where Octavia could purchase the item.

"The jeans store," she texted. *"At Garden Carcass Mall."*

Octavia exclusively wore jeans, and she'd never heard about this store. Maybe it was new. Octavia really only ever came to the mall to get Auntie Anne's and to buy her monthly BigGirlPlus Coffin-Ready underwear from the Obese Auntware department in the basement of Macy's.

Octavia looked at the thread again.

"Your hefty ass will feel like a new woman with jeans cream."

Ray really did read like she was pitching this product, and she was totally the type of gal pal who'd try to push like Avon or Weightloss Shakes on you. Try to make it seem like you're a loser if you don't sign up, and also that you'll keep being a loser even if you do. It was part of her charm.

Octavia had asked if jeans cream did something good for bigger women, like did it make jeans fit better or something.

"You have to buy your right size," Ray had typed. *"If you are size H, then you buy size H. No amount of jeans cream is going to make you size G or F if you're currently at H."*

What was size G and F and H? Octavia pondered. Was that something? She made a note to ask about this at the jeans store. Maybe they would know. But she didn't trust Ray to provide a complete, satisfying answer, so she did not bother to continue the conversation. It was possible Ray was a bit retarded but she was attractive and tall so you didn't really notice it too much. And she spoke properly, though sometimes she didn't know words and would make up replacements instead. Like one time she didn't know "specifics" so she said "mustafutts". And when Octavia asked her to repeat herself she said "mustafutts" again, when it was clearly "specifics" that she had wanted to say...

Octavia sat on the toilet, her butt a wreck, her anus pulsating with fever, and she pondered. She couldn't decide if it was worth it to text Ray and ask where exactly in the mall the Jeans Store was located. It was pretty lazy of her. She could just walk around and look, or find the directory and locate it from there. Really, she was scared of texting and not getting an immediate reply. She didn't usually text her fuck buddies questions they had to instantly respond to. It was too much pressure, too much commitment.

Octavia decided to go it on her own. She couldn't bear to text this broad and not receive a response like instantly back. Her armpits were musty just thinking about it. It was too much too soon. Octavia didn't even like texting her son questions she needed him to reply to semi-immediately. She was too shy for this type of thing. She felt loose and weird and desperate during these moments. Alone and afraid and damp in all the worst places.

After poorly wiping her ass with the rough, incompetent toilet paper in the Garden Carcass Mall Food Court Bathroom For Handicaps Only!!!, Octavia flushed the toilet with the gummy bottom of her shoe, in a damp depression, and then she used the shoe to kick at the lock of the door several times before it unlatched and the door could open.

She walked up to the sink in the bathroom and there was a baby lying there, on the sodden counter, unattended.

Octavia looked at the baby. It was silent mostly, except for some gurgling. It looked at her and flailed its arms about. Not in a panicked way, but just for something to do, it seemed.

The baby's head was disproportionately large, as if the symptom of some grim disease. The baby didn't look sick, but its head was too big. Octavia wondered how the baby could hold its head up when eighty percent of its weight was at the top. It didn't make sense, like, scientifically. And Octavia wasn't one for gravity, but some things just don't work - it's that simple.

"Where's your mom?" Octavia asked the kid. It was a white baby, so she wasn't overly concerned. It was more of a casual question, and if the baby didn't respond, she would finish washing her hands and then continue about her day.

The baby looked at her and gurgled something. He didn't seem too much concerned himself. Maybe he was from the bathroom, born there.

"Hey," a man said, stepping into view, materializing from nowhere, "are you trying to steal my kid?"

Octavia finished washing her hands. She didn't look at the man. Something about his voice was annoying to her and she knew if she looked at him and saw his face she'd grow more irritated. She walked over to the dryer area but it was towel paper instead of the hand dryer thing and Octavia grew furious that she had to reach up and take out some sheets to dry her hands instead of getting the quick, convenient, diseased air she was accustomed to in dingy, homeless-house, public restrooms.

"Hey, he's not for sale!" the man was shouting to Octavia's back as she stood in a vacuum of depression and total silence, zoned out, mechanically drying her hands. When she came to, she saw the man was in her line of sight and she was forced to see him.

The man took a step that made it clear he was meaning for her to see him, to look at and acknowledge him. She thought of Phil and felt sick. In the beginning, when Amander was having Phil around saying he was her new boyfriend, having him in Octavia and Philly's face like he was going to be a new member of the crew, Octavia ignored him. She did not like the cut of his jib. She thought he was gross; reminded her of old mustard. She wanted him gone, dead. But she wasn't going to kill anyone or even think about it. She wasn't Amander. So she would just act as if Phil wasn't there. She didn't think anything of it. Phil would be gone soon. Who *keeps* a boyfriend? This was before Octavia, who mentally was in LesboWorld at all times–This was before she understood the silly straight girls. Not only did Amander keep this dusty binch, she married him and had a fucking kid! She made a whole life with someone who was born in Canada and had a disease, on the record books, called Flattened Buttocks Syndrome! And Amander not only did all this with Phil, but she forced Octavia and Philly, and then later Nic and Leece, to be cool with it. Not only act like it, but become it.

Octavia snapped-to and screamed at the man to get away from her or she was going to kick his head in. “I’ve got my diabetes shoes on and I will use them to kick your skull right the fuck in!”

It was what she wanted to say to Phil, but it was this man who got it instead and when Octavia realized she felt deflated and hopeless.

The man was crying now. The baby looked with boredom upon the scene and Octavia felt awkward for screaming at its dad or captor or whatever.

She kicked lightly at the man who was now crumpled to the floor and he flinched at the delicate touch of her shoe.

“Hey,” she kicked him again and he flinched again.

“Where’s the jeans store?” she asked his fetal form.

The man looked up at her and said in a tired voice that it was by the dumpsters, the new annex they added on to put all the garbage and storage. It would look like it was just dumpsters, but just beyond, Octavia would see there were doors and you go in them and that’s the jeans store. It would smell like garbage but mostly it would be jeans.

“Oh, okay, thanks,” she said, still feeling weird. His body was small and formed like a woman’s. Maybe it was a woman and not a man.

The man or strange woman sat up lightly on the floor. They said, “I’ll give you the kid for twenty. Knock off ten bucks.”

Octavia waved them off, “No thanks, I already got a kid.”

“Fifteen!” it screamed to her retreating form.

Octavia wondered why she would pay to have a kid. It should be the reverse. He should be paying her. He wants to dump his kid off but *she* has to pay to relieve him of his responsibilities? Octavia wondered if she was being political. Then she wondered how far away the dumpsters were, scientifically. She was not about to walk all the way to the other side of the mall, so she went over to the security booth and took one of the scooters. The security man sitting in the booth next to the scooters said weakly to her, "Hey", like trying to tell her to stop, but that's about all he did. He was ancient, at least 90, and you could see he was partially blind. He wasn't about to run because his legs were in a cast. It'd take him twenty minutes probably just to stand up from his chair. So Octavia took off!

Octavia rolled herself to the new annex that was just a bit of building where they had all the garbage.

Strange, Octavia thought.

But just like the bathroom man said, just beyond the dumpsters and piles of trash, were two doors, and above the doors hung a white sheet. Octavia squinted and she could see someone had tried to write "Jeans Store" in normal penmanship, in regular marker, onto the sheet. The sign was not readable to anyone casually strolling by or really even to someone like Octavia who was purposely looking for the store, thus rendering the effectiveness of the sign a mostly-flop. But it was the thought that counted in most cases, though Octavia felt, personally, it was the follow-through that counted more than anything, in almost every instance of anything that has ever happened, or not happened.

Octavia parked her scooter (it was hers now and she planned to take it home with her from the mall) at back of one of the hulking dumpsters. The dumpster in question was spilling over with Chinese mannequins and she knew it was from that store that sold live dogs in plastic bags like goldfish.

Octavia moved herself from the dumpster and then had to climb over a bunch of garbage bags to get over by the Jeans Store door. She was shocked when she heard a voice go, "We have the new Karate Jeans in," and then the person belonging to the voice handed her a sheet of paper that just said “Karate Jeans” on it and nothing else.

It was a man standing by the door, squeezed tight behind a great pile of trash. Octavia figured he was one of the Jeans Store employees who had been delegated to handing-out-flyers duty. Octavia felt sad for him, so said, “Karate Jeans, huh?”

“Yeah, *Karate Jeans*,” he spat.

Octavia instantly regretted trying to validate his meaningless existence by pretending to be interested in whatever karate jeans were. The name actually explained itself, to be honest. Much more so than Jeans Cream ever could.

Octavia didn’t know why she kept talking to him instead of moving on into the store, but she said, “So they are jeans you wear when you do karate?”

“Pretty much,” he said with an attitude. Octavia thought how his mission was to sell whomever came to the door on the new jeans. He needed to convince every person coming into the store that they needed a pair. He didn’t seem especially interested in pushing the product on Octavia, and she took offense. Did she not seem like someone who would be interested in karate jeans? Was it an insult if he thought that or was it actually a sign she was on the right path that he felt trying to sell her on these things was a waste of time?

“They’re for the serious karate guy. The guy who’ll go to a discotheque and bust out a can of whoop ass if someone spikes his drink. If someone tries to date-rape a glamorous man at a speakeasy and he’s wearing his karate jeans he won’t have any issue getting that leg up for a roundhouse or ax-kick to the dome, believe you me.”

Octavia nodded like she was really impressed and interested. *“Huh,”* she said, like it was all so fascinating, and the man rolled his eyes.

"They're just jeans," he said, using a different voice now, and Octavia realized his dispassionate tone throughout had nothing to do with her. He was just depressed with his shitty life and upon the realization of this Octavia's anxiety instantly melted away and she moved to feeling warmed-over, at peace and content. Everything was going to be okay.

"They're jeans and they're a bit stretchy and very snug to the form," he went on. "So if you're a karate man, and you want to go to a night club but are afraid of being raped, these are the good jeans to buy because they're hard to take off."

Octavia didn't know why out of her mouth came, "The rapist could just use a knife and cut a hole into the butt of the jeans - if that is what they really want to do."

The man looked at her, thinking. "I suppose," he nodded.

"Is the material thick?" Octavia pressed.

The man thought for a moment. "Not like the carpenter jeans." Then he gestured to Octavia's GirlPlus MissBig-sized FUBU jeans, "Not like those, no. Thinner material; a lycra blend, maybe. Sturdy, but probably pretty rippable if a knife or sword is involved." The man looked at Octavia's jeans in a deeper sense, then said, "Yeah, you wouldn't get raped in those. No one would want to, anyway."

Octavia felt pleased with his response. She nodded, bidding adieu to the gentleman, and then proceeded on into the store.

Right up in front, as soon as you walked in, was a taxidermy deer. It looked like a real deer at first and Octavia shouted expletives when she saw it, afraid, but then she looked and saw it was stiff and unmoving, but still wasn't completely sure until she walked up to and then around it, studying the beast, and saw it was not alive. Killed and stuffed and propped up in this jeans emporium to scare people into shitting in their pants so they're forced to buy new ones from the store.

They think they're slick, Octavia thought about the jeans store merchants. She almost turned around to leave, irritated, when she saw, right behind the deer, was a display with a bunch of unlabeled tubes scattered about.

Is this jeans cream? Octavia wondered.

A woman materialized, like the man from the bathroom. Long red acrylics and the sound of jingling keys. Her titties were out. Not all the way, but most of her bosom was hanging out. You couldn't see the nipple, but just about. Octavia's eyes went right to the bosom, and right on the woman's right titty was a nametag: *Janet*.

She gestured to the display of tubes with her talons and it made a light clacking noise even though she hadn't touched anything.

"Jeans cream?" Janet said. Her voice was creamy and wet-sounding. Jeans creamy and wet sounding.

Octavia moved forward, to get her nose and forehead closer to the bosom, to catch its heat, but also to get a closer look at the tubes.

"This is jeans cream?" Octavia said, studying the hoard, then looking up quickly into Janet's bosom, then under her chin that was sprinkled with hundreds of little hairs some long and thin and some short and thick and spiked, and then she looked up into Janet's face which was wet with dew, and old and sick-looking.

"Indeed," Janet creamed.

All at once, Octavia noticed how quiet and still the store was. Octavia understood it was only Janet, and only her. She stood up from the jeans cream display, and didn't know what she wanted to do next. She noticed the store was darkened all around. The only light that came in was from the outside, out by the where the dumpsters and garbage were and much of that light was blocked off because of it. So there was a small sliver coming in through the front glass doors, or maybe plastic doors, and they hit mostly on the deer, and then a bit of it spread to the jeans cream display where they were standing just beyond. But the rest of the store was completely dark, as if it were closed. No one knew about this store, only freaks, Octavia thought. Ray, who was retarded or mentally ill or both; the man from the bathroom with that sodden baby; and Janet, with her bosom and chin hairs who looked in the face like she had died and had her post-corpse makeup slathered together by some demented mortician. Then something weird happened with witchcraft or a mad scientist got involved and she was brought back alive to go out into the world to hawk the mysterious jeans cream.

Octavia looked at the tubes again, then said to Janet, who just stared as if she were casually watching a film, "Do you make this cream?"

Janet opened her mouth and it sounded like macaroni and cheese being stirred in a pot. She took forever to speak, her mouth just hanging open, strings of spit going from the top of her lip to the bottom. When she did speak, she said, "They are sent to us."

"Well what does it do?"

Janet moved to pick up a tube and when she did, Octavia jerked despite herself. She was afraid, or turned on. The same things, really.

"You need the jeans cream," Janet said, holding the tube as if she were a host on QVC. "It has restorative properties."

Octavia just looked at her. Her skin was the texture and color of a raw, expired chicken.

At last, she said, “Does that answer my question, though?.. What is it restoring?”

“The jeans,” Janet said, “And you in the jeans. By the grace of the Lord.”

Some hippie shit, Octavia thought with skepticism. Of course this was some weirdo hotepish shit the contemptible whore Ray would be into. A cream that healed you and your jeans. It was very Instagram slut. Ray had like 30k followers on instagram and one time was flown out to Dubai by an accountant for some wealthy arab sheik and he paid her like fifteen thousand dollars to shit in his mouth. Octavia had thought that was a hefty dollar amount to fork over for such a thing. She would pay like ten dollars for that, at best. Octavia wondered briefly if she was jealous of Ray. Did she want to be her, or poop in her mouth? She thought, wouldn’t it be easier to be the person so taken under by the concept of mysterious jeans cream? It would be an easier life. A happier one, though one likely to end very shortly from overwhelming stupidity.

“Okay,” Octavia said too loudly, too brightly to Janet, who winced at the sudden volume. “I’ll take a tube! How much?”

Janet winced once again, because Octavia was literally shouting into her face.

“Seventy dollars,” Janet answered, and she stared.

Octavia at once thought that the cream, in its basic tube form, was far too expensive but also she was surprised it was so cheap. Stuff like this, random mysterious goo, usually started in the hundreds. It was the promises you were buying, and delusions aren’t cheap.

Octavia handed over her Discover Platinum (*that’s right*) Card.

“Seventy dollars, it is!” she cheesed, and regretted it.

Janet creamily took the card from Octavia's grasp and held it, looking at it. She said, "Do we have a machine?" and looked voided into Octavia's face. Something in Janet was falling apart, falling away. Something was dying and fading out.

"H–" Octavia started, and she looked at Janet, who seemed to be sinking into herself. "How would I know if you have a machine? *What* machine?" Octavia looked around, she had returned to herself, and was back to being afraid. Or had never not been afraid, but was more normal afraid now. She was off the dubai shitting thing and now back into the real world and she was cold and alone, once again. Cold and alone, and with Janet, who would suck her in deeper somewhere, somewhere darker and more unknown.

She looked at Janet. "Do you work here?"

Janet nodded dumbly, then she reached to hand Octavia one of the unmarked tubes. It looked like a tube of toothpaste that someone had slapped a blank label onto.

Octavia took the tube. Janet was just standing there slack-jawed, still holding Octavia's Discover Platinum Card. Octavia considered just snatching her card back without having paid, and then running (or briskly shuffling) to the door and leaving and hopping onto her scooter and getting away with a crime, scot-free.

Janet wouldn't chase her. Janet wasn't cognizant. She wasn't aware of the world itself, only her little space behind the Jeans Cream display. So, with that in mind, Octavia made a run for it. And just as she thought, Janet did not give chase, and Octavia was able to get away with a free seventy dollar jeans cream tube, and there would be no consequence. She had a free scooter now, too. She thought about giving it to Octavian for Christmas instead of what he asked for in his letter to Santa. *"I wish my daddy loved me. Can you bring him back?"*. That was a ridiculous thing to ask of Santa, anyway. He only trafficked in material goods. Octavia wondered if her son was mentally delayed.

—

The day of the trip, Octavia went out to brunch with Nic and Leece before heading over to the Grey Butt Bus depot to board for Florida.

Nic and Leece were the Brunch Girls. They had brunch every day, no matter what was going on. Nic had brunch, provocatively, the mornings of and after 9/11. She had brunch during her father's funeral. It was being held in a church right across the street from Waffle House. She popped in briefly to make sure he was well and properly deceased, then she popped right back out and headed across the street in her fuzzy Adidas slides to get hash browns and a chicken melt.

Nic wasn't playing about brunch. Leece was more flexible on the general brunch subject. She wasn't as serious. She enjoyed the freedoms of being childfree and never having a man. Before Nic came into her life, Leece would be prone to waking up at two or three in the afternoon just because she could. She didn't have responsibilities. She often had a job that started in the morning but if she slept through her alarm and did not turn up for her shift and was fired it didn't really matter. She could just get another job, or not. She had no one to support or look after besides herself and that allowed her to care very little about any matter every second.

She got really into the Brunch Lifestyle once Nic came around. The Brunch set and aesthetic inspired Leece. She liked how embracing the Brunch scene made her general buminess seem glamorous, like she was one of those terrible hags from *Sex and the City* or something. It actually motivated her to start waking up before the sun began to wane so she could get over to Papas Fritas before eleven am for bottomless mimosas.

She didn't even like mimosas, but she looked fun and free when she drank them. Nic and her various Brunching Affiliates would often take a ton of photos of Brunch Fun, at first for Myspace, then Facebook, then Instagram and now HornyMatureWomen.viv, which was the new popular site to post highly curated fleeting snapshots of your incredibly dismal life except in the snapshot you are sipping carefree on a champagne flute full of vodka and there is a bit of Sunny Delight splashed in for aesthetic purposes so you look super like rich and totally HIV-free. Carefree and fun and faboo!

Leece liked how embracing Brunch made it seem like she was really living it up. Especially because she wasn't at all. After brunch she'd go right back home and get under the covers and sleep until it was dark time, then wake up and have a microwaved Hungry Man dinner or get door dashed Long John Silvers if she was feeling fancy. Then she'd watch cartoons for like eight hours after that until she passed out on the futon she still hadn't converted into a real couch because what was the point of real furniture. She never invited anyone up to her apartment. It was too small. Too small to bring men for sex. They would have to hunch her with their knees pushed up to their chest if they wanted to do creampies in her loft bed. And she didn't bring friends over because she didn't really like them. She didn't want them in her house. Especially Octavia because she had dreads. She didn't want crumbles of dread hair all over her one duvet set that she was still using from college.

Brunch was fun for Leece, but if Nic succumbed to her HIV and Leece got dumped from the Brunch scene, Leece would just go back to sleeping in until the wee hours of the afternoon and then waking up and immediately having half a box of donuts. The only difference between that grim option and her current Brunch lifestyle were the shockingly volatile photoshoots that'd happen every Brunch and the watery, disgusting mimosas that symbolized vitality and spry. But the photos and splash of orange juice was just that - symbols. It was just fun to pretend and appear to have things in a purely superficial sense, but Leece didn't really need the validation of Brunch. Nic did though because she had HIV.

Octavia poked at some green gloop on her plate, “What is this?”

Leece was scarfing down her breakfast burrito which was two large pancakes wrapped around a handful of sausage patties, scrambled egg, bacon, hashbrown rounds and the sauce to hold it all together was syrup. Nic had made fun of Leece for ordering such a hungry man, greedy ass meal. Leece had said, “You have HIV.”

Octavia, who didn’t really like to overly indulge right before getting on any bus, had made an attempt to get something light and breezy so she wouldn’t have to poop a bunch on a bus toilet that’s like two fucking inches from someone’s seat and head. She had chosen something called Skinty Girl Brekkie, thinking it’d be some light salad or some shit. When the plate came out it was just a bunch of brown and green piles of gloop. It made her feel sick and like she was eating out of a toilet. Octavia vowed never to do brunch again. She had no idea why she hung out with someone who had HIV and someone who had taken less dick than Octavia and she was a fucking lesbian. *Learn something from this,* Octavia chastised herself.

“I don’t know,” Leece said, her mouth full of sausage and pancake, her arms and elbows on the table, hunched over her plate like an animal. “Some vegan shit probably.”

Octavia shook her large head, despondent. “Tired of this.”

Nic laughed, spraying food, and Leece screamed because some bits of food had gone from Nic’s mouth onto Leece’s face by her eye.

“It literally looks like shit,” Nic was saying, pointing at Octavia’s plate, laughing. “It looks like baby shit.”

“It got on me,” Leece said in a strained voice to Octavia, shaking, vainly wiping at her eye.

Octavia opened her LesbianPlus wallet and pulled out a small sachet of DUDE WIPES, which are like little hand wipes for dudes. Like for when you eat barbecue or get poop on your hands in a public bathroom and can't rush home right away immediately to scrub down with lye.

She handed a wipe to Leece. "Just wipe it off."

"It's already gotten in me, I'm infected," Leece said, trembling. Her hand was shaking as she moved mechanically to wipe her face, though she'd already wiped it, and if she was infected, she was infected. The wipe might mush it in more, Octavia thought, and she waited, and watched.

Interrupting Octavia's patient observing of the situation with Leece, Nic was saying to Octavia, "What's the tea with your girl, Amander? Why is she texting me asking if you have a problem?"

Octavia looked at Nic. She looked so happy that it was Octavia who was the current object of Amander's ire. But Octavia thought Nic to be a fool. *Me today and you tomorrow.* She wasn't even thinking this in a hopeful or resentful way, it was just the way it was. Never get comfortable and confident, and never celebrate others' misfortune because it will be you next, and you won't be laughing.

Octavia just rolled her eyes, then regretted it. Nic was the type to snitch to Amander that she had rolled her eyes and Octavia'd be getting texts from Amander reminding Octavia that Amander had a uncle in the CIA, and a halfbrother in ISIS. Like somebody was supposed to be scared of that. Octavia had a cousin who had his hand up the ass of one of the lesser-known puppets on *Sesame Street.* She could do threats, too.

Octavia stuck a fork into an item on her plate that looked like a hush puppy that had been fried in the vat for like thirty hours. She thought, okay, something I can maybe sink my teeth into. But when she went to stab her fork into the thing it was soft and mushy, like some sort of sponge cake and Octavia felt sick. *What is this,* she screamed internally. Inside the mush were a bunch of seeds. It activated her trypophobia and made her sick. She closed her eyes quickly, and with her eyes closed, started smashing hard on the thing to conceal all the little seeds and get her brain to stop popping and making her itch.

Octavia realized she had fallen away from the table into the abyss and brought herself back together to say to Nic, who had been looking on at Octavia having her little freak-out over the hushpuppy with mostly incurious indifference, sighing, "Amander said Phil's bringing a pal."

"Jesus, like some little boy he is dating?" Nic said for some reason.

Leece laughed, spitting out the mimosa milkshake she'd ordered right before complaining her stomach had been fucked up for months because she'd been doing a brussel sprouts-exclusive diet to lose a bit of weight, to look better in her Brunch photos, and she had almost shitted herself to death. Still in recovery, her dumb ass orders a mimosa milkshake and five pound Brekkie Burrrito at ten in the morning on a raw, ruined stomach.

"Noo?" Octavia said in her r u dumb tone to Nic. "Worse, actually. Some friend he made doing his soup reviews. I guess it's a fellow soup reviewer. Yoshi Hashimoto."

"What the fuck?" Nic said, shocked.

"Yeah, I know," Octavia was like.

"What is he like…" Nic moved her head lower to the table, closer, so only they could hear, *"oriental?"*

Octavia shrugged. "I mean, might as well be, right? Imagine someone Phil of all creatures would befriend. This freak–I mean, him being Japanese or some shit is likely the least of our concerns."

Leece offered a neutral opinion. "I can't believe Phil has a friend."

“Imagine how fucking down bad you have to be to end up as a friend of Phil’s,” Octavia offered as a compliment to anyone who wasn’t Yoshi Hashimoto.

“Well, he’s Asian,” Leece reminded her.

“That’s messed up,” Nic said, and then she hit her fork on Octavia’s arm, and Octavia was glad she was wearing her Super Thick Sleeve BigGirlPlus FUBU Carpenter Jean Shirt. She figured she was safe from having absorbed any…microbes that might have been on the fork.

“So *what did you do?* Why is Mr. Mander upset with bestie?” Nic was glowing with glee at Octavia being out of favor with Amander, a rare occurrence.

Octavia thought how Nic was the least liked, openly, in the crew, and specifically by Amander, who thought the only thing Nic had to offer was “nice earlobes”.

“I’d cut them off and sell them on the dark web if you guys would let go of your pathetic obsession with and insistence on having at least one traditionally pretty girl in the Book Group.”

Amander called their friendship the “Book Group”. They did read books sometimes. Octavia often used them to workshop her material. They read Harry Potter once (*“I’d kill all these demonic little kids,”* was Leece’s contribution. *“I’d lock up Hogwarts and set it on fire with all of them trapped inside”*. Everyone had agreed.).

Octavia thought how they all called Nic Niggarette behind her back because her full name was Nicarette and so it was a little play on the name there. Nig was never included in the book club aspect of their crew.

"Can someone who got fired from Pathmark for stealing Peeps even blink without assistance? Never mind *read?*" was Amander's reasoning for why Nic was not included to read Old Yeller and things of that nature with them.

Nic knew Amander didn't like her. Nic was only in the group because Octavia had wanted to smash all those years ago, and still did, though it was clear at this point that was never going to happen, at least not until Nic got really desperate or something and she already had HIV and a boyfriend who worked at Subway and on his BlackPeopleMeet profile it said "dedicated sandwich artist" and she was the one who had initiated the relationship, even though she saw that sandwich artist thing clear as day, so it was looking like a down bad, will-do-anything-just-to-feel Nic wasn't appearing anytime soon, but they were all too lazy to kick her out, except for Amander, who had no issue making shit shake, but for some odd reason she seemed to need the approval and permission of the rest of the group to carry out her diabolical little plans. Just like a demon, Leece had said once. Octavia thought: Yes, angry and hot. And that was when she realized she might be attracted to Amander. She had always been from the beginning. And that ugly idiot Phil was in the way. If Amander would date a subhumanoidal mongoloid like Phil, Octavia was sure she would consider doing lesbo stuff, even just in secret. If only Phil would go.

Octavia explained to Nic and Leece about what had happened at the Garden Carcass Mall with Phil.

"Have you read his soup reviews?" Nic said in a scandalized voice, raising a concerned brow. "It's elder abuse to publish those things. I read a review he did for Minestrone and almost cried from how angry it made me. Like, I was *shaking*." ("You have HIV," Leece explained.) "It was like a whole page of droning on about all the different beans. They shouldn't be able to inflict that kind of thing on the elderly. They'll stroke out or something."

"Maybe that's the plan," Octavia responded absentmindedly, poking at the newborn diarrhea that'd been splattered on her plate in a fanciful manner. She wasn't interested in the conversation. She didn't want to talk about

Phil. She always tried so hard to just look away from him and make him disappear in her mind, and from existence.

"Oh, Miss Conspiracy Theory over here!" Nic said, guffawing, making a big display.

Leece said, "Nic, where were you yesterday? I waited for you forever outside of Walgreens. I thought you needed Blistex?"

Nic got cold, uncomfortable. "I was having lab work done..."

Leece cut her eyes to Octavia and Octavia had to pull her moustache in by her teeth to keep from laughing.

As Leece was saying with a jaunty look on her face to Nic, *"What were the results?"*, suddenly a man was at the side of their table. He looked like a Ninja Turtle. It was an acceptable Lesbian category, but not an acceptable Hetero Male category. It wasn't okay to be, as a straight man seeking women, a ninja turtle person.

The man was as tall as a tall third grader. He had one of those hard muscle bodies. His neck had all this shit at the back. It made Octavia wonder what you had to do at the gym to beef up your neck muscles like that. How do you do the weights there? Octavia had never seen the inside of a gym. She had never been to or walked by one. It was another one of those things that she thought was just in movies. Do running and movements and shit *on purpose? And you pay?* What the fuck.

The man licked his lips and made these grotesque mouth sounds–it was like his tongue made a noise when it moved–and he said, *"Good morning,"* in an affected deep and sexy voice, only to Leece.

Nic snorted and some of her HIV snot got on the table.

Octavia was, at once, transfixed on the scene. She felt bad, but she loved when one of the girls got approached by a man. It was like watching a horror film but in person. It was so cringe and horrible and made her skin crawl and she loved every minute of it. She loved that it was happening to them and not to her. That she could merely observe. She could still experience all the horrible feelings, but after it was over, she could go back to normal, fine. But the victim, they were scarred permanently. Octavia secretly liked that part the best. It ensured many more moments like this occurring in the future. These moments, these men, they beat the gals down, bit by bit. Then they were ruined, slowly over time, and it left them vulnerable for more, for worse.

Leece always had these creatures coming up to her. While Nic was the certified "pretty one", Leece was attractive in her own right. She was tall and shapely and had big lips and gigantic thighs. She swished and swayed. But Octavia thought Leece attracted men the most because she hated them. Though Leece was constantly going on dates, she wasn't as desperate as she tried to lead the other girls into believing. Always complaining about being single and not getting enough creampies. But Leece was symmetrical and normal-seeming enough to have a man if she wanted one, but she never did. The men could sense she didn't particularly care for them as a genre, and that was dognip.

"No, too short," Leece said without looking at the man, dismissing him.

Octavia had to fight back snorting globs of snot out like Nic. It was one thing for Nic, who had HIV, to be all a chuckle. But if the Man Hating Lesbian laughed, the scene would be cut short at once, and Octavia would be disappointed.

"Excuse me, beautiful," the man said, unfazed. Octavia loved this, when they kept on even after one of the girls made clear their disinterest. Really, a passionate disgust. Much more clear than just your general lack of interest. The disgust seemed to motivate the men. They appeared to be under the assumption they could "prove" the woman wrong, and that the interaction needed to be dominated, no matter the direction or tone, and that they, the man, could and would “win”.

The man started to talk again but Leece waved her hand in a dismissive fashion, annoyed, “I'm taller than you.”

And she was, by like a lot. Even with Leece sitting down you could tell she had like a foot on him and Octavia was about to piss herself it was so fucking funny.

Nic was on her side of the table dying laughing into her napkin, thankfully containing her mucus to the closed system of thick ass brunch restaurant/tapas and jazz infusion bar at night cloth napkins.

“Vindicated” by Dashboard Confessional blared aggressively through the Papas Fritas restaurant speakers.

The man said to Leece, “So?”. He was wearing a baseball cap and one of those beach muscles tank tops that show you the underside of the man titty.

Leece said to his pathetic “so?”, “So, I'm taller than you. Scram.”

“I could be your soulmate,” the man countered, but it wasn't romantic, or him trying to be romantic. He had an attitude and said it in a butt-puckered, sassy ass voice.

Leece leaned over to him, for the first time fully acknowledging him with her eyes. She gritted her teeth, bared them, and showed all the sausage and pancake bits bursting through the spaces in between and she said, her jaw tight, her voice a low growl, *“Get, beast.”*

The man started getting upset. He said, “Okay, but can you answer my question?”

“You didn’t ask a question, troll,” Leece said, losing interest in scaring him.

He was using a whiny, clawing voice when he said, “What if I was your soulmate? That’s how you're gonna do me?”

Leece dismissed him with, “My soulmate isn’t a midget.”

The man was getting wet on his face and his neck veins were bursting and they looked like viruses, little worms, “You wanna know why I'm short? Because my dad fucked my *short mom*, because that’s what men are attracted to, so good luck finding someone to climb that tree!”

He was foaming at the corner of his mouth when he huffed off, and Leece waved her hand in a fluttery way to his retreating form and called, “Bye, goblin!”

Nic was cracking up inconsolable as Leece turned to Octavia, saying, “It was weird how he mentioned his parents’ sex life.”

“Probably watches them,” Octavia offered and Leece chuckled.

“I can hear my auntie now, ‘*This is why you don’t have a man’*. Like, okay? I’m not dating a fucking little person.”

“I think that might be ableist,” Octavia said, warm and aglow from such a pleasurable experience.

“Is being small a disability?” Leece scoffed. “Everything is a disability now. I was on a date with this guy last week who said he had a chronic peeing disease.”

“Overactive bladder?”

Leece reacted in disgust, like she thought it was so put upon. “Whatever, like this nigga was drinking mad soda. *On a date at a nice restaurant*. He had like eight coca colas. I'm like the fuck you drinking all that soda for? And this was after he told me about his pissing disease. Let me tell you why your stupid ass is constantly going to the bathroom."

Nic was dying laughing. *"Eight sodas?"*

Leece nodded, annoyed at the memory, "Yeah, *mad sodas*. I'm sitting there like what the fuck."

Nic wiped tears from her eyes, still laughing. "Your life is so tragic."

"..You literally have HIV?" Leece looked to Octavia like is she serious and Octavia couldn't help it and laughed.

Leece went to grab her bottle of water, a Dasani, but paused as she brought it to her lips. She extended her arm from her face and examined the bottle from a distance.

"I wouldn't drink that," Ock warned, "It's pool water."

Leece looked at her, "So you was just gon' watch and let me get the bottle all the way up to my lip before you said something."

Octavia's response was, "You're forty-one. I shouldn't have to tell you about Dasani, you should already know this."

Leece ignored the criticism and moved her eyes back to the blue bottle, in shock and genuine awe. She twisted the bottle around her grasp in disgust, "Like, what are these paper bits??". She took a swig anyway, and said after she was finished, "I been swallowed like mad pool water from when I used to go to the YMCA for day camp after school, so it's whatever."

"This is why you don't have a man," Octavia joked, prompting Leece to fling some of the Dasani water at her face, which prompted Octavia to shriek in horror.

After the scene, Nic was shaking her head, saying she couldn't believe Philly had named her daughter after a bottle of drinkable ammonia.

Ock said, "I think her dad Jafar named her that?"

"Is that what that nigga's name is?" Leece laughed, genuinely surprised. "I thought Dasani's dad was named Ricardo. I don't know why I thought he was Mexican or some shit. Dasani got that wide ass torso and Toucan Sam hooked-over ass bird beak, so I just assumed."

"Should you be speaking about your niece like that?" Nic was saying as Ock was correcting Leece with, "Jafar is from Turkey. You should probably know the bare minimum basic facts about people you're literally related to."

Leece blinked, unable to compute.

"Wait, like, a turkey giveaway?" Nic was saying, confused. She had met her last boyfriend at a turkey giveaway being held at the YMCA where Philly's man Demarcus worked as a "personal trainer" and "part time janitor". They didn't provide gloves for him to use while he cleaned, but they said he could just buy some little ziploc baggies and put them on his hands and then tie them off with a rubber band or one of those twisty ties they put on bread. Philly had said she asked Demarcus why he couldn't just buy gloves. Demarcus said he wasn't too much concerned about it. "I prefer to freehand it, anyway," Philly had told them he said, and they all imagined Demarcus wiping shit off the YMCA bathroom walls with just his bare hands and some silky ass motel soap.

"Noo," Octavia looked at Nic in disgust. "Like Turkey the country, or whatever it is. The place. Not a turkey giveaway. No one gets a man from a turkey giveaway except you."

While Leece was busy snort-laughing, Nic was defending herself, saying, "Lots of fine ass men at a free turkey giveaway."

Octavia shook her dreads, “Aint nothin’ fine about standing in line for free turkey. Only *you* tryna get fucked in that scenario.” Octavia looked at her severely, serious, “Understand that.”

While Leece was laughing, Nic was busy disagreeing, saying, “You’re at the river dunking your paw into the stream for salmon and shit. You don’t have a clue about what women who want dick are interested in, no offense. You don’t know this world.”

Leece quickly cut in to say, “I only take dick and I would never look for a man at the YMCA (subtle Philly shade), or at a free turkey giveaway. It’s never that serious.”

“It’s never that serious, but you never have a man. Maybe if your busted, lonely ass was more open-minded you’d have someone to share your bed with at night.”

Leece countered with, “I sleep in a four poster twin sized bed so only me fits?”

Octavia laughed and said they were both trash.

Leece looked at her, saying, “A bitch who got HIV tryna tell me how to live.”

Octavia cackled wildly, despite herself.

“The first time I take advice from a bitch who got HIV will be the motherfucking *last time*, because within the week I’m liable to be fucking deceased. Thanks but no thanks.” And then Leece obnoxiously cacawed and they were asked to leave the restaurant.

Walking onto the Grey Butt Bus, Octavia was stopped by a bulky wheelchair blocking the aisle leading to the seats. The woman, whom Octavia instantly clocked as Mary's cousin Yolanda, yes, looked exactly like Luther Vandross in the face.

Yolanda was saying to Mary, who was seated in one of the front seats, adjacent to Yolanda's chair in the aisle, "Cuz God don't play about me!"

Mary looked with disinterest at her cousin, saying, "I don't think God cares for you at all. You're in a wheelchair. You gotta use an oxygen tank. How are you even still alive?"

Octavia looked at the oxygen tank sutured to the side of Yolanda's old timey wheelchair. The chair part was like a weaved basket. It looked like some rickety shit Franklin D. Roosevelt would be scootin' around in.

Yolanda closed her eyes, her lids crusted with dried mucus, and she said smugly, "By the grace of God, that's how."

Mary sucked her teeth, unconvinced, "Why did God allow slavery?"

Yolanda looked serious, serene, "Why does God do anything? He has his reasons."

"Okay and what are they?" Mary asked with wide-eyed disgust.

"It's not for you to know, your only job is to believe."

Mary sucked her teeth, "Okay, well, I *believe* he is a rude idiot."

Yolanda nodded solemnly and then breathed in a composed, neutered way like a nun. Leece, who had been standing behind Octavia, impatiently waiting to get to her seat, moved forward and kicked her Timb at Yolanda's wheelchair.

"Ayo, move this wheelchair! Sit in the handicapped section, idiot!"

Yolanda, unmoved, told Leece there was no handicap section on the Grey Butt Bus.

"So you sit your bulky shit in the middle of the aisle and the rest of us are supposed to - *what?*"

Yolanda just shrugged. So Leece, enraged, pushed forward and started kicking at the wheelchair until it moved enough that she could squeeze through to down the aisle. Octavia just stood there and waited, glad Leece was a skitch more of a piece of shit than she was, and was able to handle things in whichever way the situations required themselves to be resolved. Octavia had wanted to kick the wheelchair out of place, too, but she couldn't afford the bad karma, or ire of that famed rude idiot God. She was already lesbian. You were only allowed the one thing, and that was her thing.

Octavia was moving to follow after Leece after she'd kicked in the wheelchair, but Mary stopped her and asked Octavia when they would be arriving at their destination.

Octavia paused by the seat and looked.

"..We haven't even got moving yet.."

Mary blinked a grey eye. "Sure," she said, and some phlegmy stuff came out between the gap in her teeth and landed on a crustacean jutting out from her lip. "But when do you expect we'll touch down? Is this like a months-long journey?.. Because I only packed as much shit as my plastic ShopRite bag could hold, and if it's going to take us, like, *months* to get to this place, I don't think it's going to be enough. Do they have clothes there; water?"

Octavia just looked. When she'd given her publisher the final body count for how many Grey Butt Bus tickets she'd need, her response had been, "I'm a Toastmasters' Apprentice at Quiznos.. Where do you think I'm getting all of these tix from?"

"From the fucking ticket booth," Octavia responded. This broad was so unprofessional it was ridiculous. In the end, Octavia had to use her Discover Platinum Card to pay for half the tickets, so she ultimately had to fork over the seventy dollars she thought she'd ingeniously "saved" from stealing that tube of jeans cream from Janet. Karma never took its foot off Octavia's meaty neck. They knew about the Lesbian thing, and her *As Told By Ginger* erotic fanfiction, and she was on their list.

Octavia sighed with succulent depression.

"Bro, I don't know," Octavia said with exasperation to Mary wondering when they would reach Florida. Octavia still wasn't sure it was a real place. Mary suspected the same and seemed to be trying to "test" Octavia to see if it appeared Octavia might possess more worldly knowledge concerning such matters; see if she was hiding something, doing a trick.

"Ballpark it," Mary said, eyeing her suspiciously.

Octavia sighed, "Bro, I honestly don't even know. I doubt it takes months." She had no Earthly idea. It could take years; eons. Who the fuck has ever been to Florida? She's never met them; she doesn't know anyone who has.

Mary looked at her, "This is your <u>second</u> time calling me bro." She put up two fingers, the peace sign, a warning.

"Sir?"

Octavia felt a damp tug on her arm and looked down and it was Yolanda.

"Sir, why did your friend hurt me?"

Mary reached over to punch at Yolanda's oxygen tank, and gently corrected her cousin, saying, "It's a girl, bitch!"

Yolanda took a moment to pull back in her chair and examine Octavia more closely. She opened her mouth in an O, and said, "*Ohhh*. I see now a more female shape, perhaps. Lovely birthing hips."

Octavia just walked away from them, hearing Mary lovingly ask of her cousin "Are you a fucking retarded idiot?", and went to go find a seat away from the front with the disabled freaks whom she had invited but had forgotten why. As she moved down the aisle she was stopped instantly by Phil, who smiled at her with a mouth like a sloppy cheeseburger.

Jesus, she thought.

"It should be considered elder abuse for the Senior Citizen Gazette to be commissioning works from him," Octavia faintly heard Nic complaining about Phil in the way back. She had gotten on the bus ahead of Ock and Leece, who'd gone into the Grey Butt Bus bus station to have post-brunch explosive diarrhea before they boarded. Nic was sat next to Barb who sat still with her face drawn, exhumed. Her soul had been fumigated long ago when she became a mom, giving birth to Philly, who would go on to have three different baby daddies and one of them is named Jafar from Turkey and he was the least shittiest baby daddy. By the time Leece came sloughing out of Barb's womb she had nothing left, which explained basically everything about Leece.

Octavia liked Barb because she hated everyone in the group. She liked how Barb was only in the group because her daughters were in the group. Barb didn't like her children, and she especially didn't like their lesbian and HIV-having friends, but she was there anyway, for her daughters. Octavia thought it was cute, even though she rarely spoke to Barb, and the one time they really were sitting down and looking at each other and trying to communicate Barb said "How did you have a child? If you're…against men?" and Octavia felt like whooping her, but she couldn't because Barb was old, and Philly would get mad, and Octavia didn't feel like punching and getting sweaty and tired and then after she's calmed down she realizes she's dented some old woman's head in. That's not what Mr. Kim taught when she took his karate class at the back of the methadone clinic. You respected your fellow man, and you only busted out the nunchucks if an Indian man in flip-flops was trying to scam you into buying off-market cellphones out of the back of his Mazda hatchback. That was the only time Mr. Kim said it was okay to start beating on anyone, old or young. It seemed a bit specific, but Octavia never questioned bae.

Phil was saying, "They have complimentary Quiznos," and he held up a soggy, vomit-colored sandwich to show Ock.

Why can I see your breath more than your hairline? Octavia pondered about him, as he was putting the sandwich close up under her nose and some of it got on her.

"What is that?" Octavia asked, jerking her head away. When he put the sandwich on her it felt like a rat. She'd never felt a rat before, but when the sandwich touched her, she was certain that is what it would feel like. Kind of solid and hairy and mildly damp and a little bit greasy and round when you don't expect it and hard when you don't expect it and soft when you least expect it.

"Chicken caesar pizza," Phil answered, and he took the sandwich back to take a squishy bite of it.

"What the fuck is chicken caesar pizza?" Octavia asked, angry with how irritated she was. Her question went unanswered. Did Phil understand she had spoken? Did he think she was just speaking to speak and not demanding answers? She stood and waited, and after a while, of her just staring at Phil chewing into the sludge of his sandwich, Amander, sitting next to Phil and looking on at both of them detached, curious, said,

"He's mad at me."

Octavia turned up her face and said *"who?"* with disgust, when she knew Amander was referring to Phil.

Phil leaned over in his seat, "She forgot my parchment! How will I write?"

Octavia looked at him. He was so ugly and disgusting. There had to be something wrong with Amander to lie with a creature like this, she thought. Or, maybe Nic was right and Octavia just didn't "get" the strictly-prickly crew. Ock was down at the river molesting salmon or whatever Nic said, and *sure*, but she didn't have HIV, and she wasn't married to a purposeless peasant who writes soup reviews for people on their deathbed, the majority of whom are tubed at the stomach so what the fuck are they worried about soup??

Amander said, "I forgot his parchment."

At least, Octavia thought, she didn't seem truly upset about what she had "done". Amander seemed amused. Maybe Amander got off on torturing Phil in little ways. Octavia could see Amander being that type of wife. Marrying some poor sack just to have front-view seats to a daily trainwreck. This was kind of how Ock was with her single straight friends. She'd totes marry one of them just to have more consistent access to them and their sad threads. She could marry Nic and they could sleep in the same bed. So when Nic comes home from her depressing dates where she's gotten HIV again, or maybe something more fun like leprosy, she will tell all to Ock. It could be their nightly ritual. Ock wouldn't marry Leece because Leece seemed like the type of person who left shit chunks on the sheets. Despite having AIDS, Nic seemed pretty clean, though Octavia would make sure to put a pillow between them in the bed, you know, just to be safe.

"How will I write?" Phil cried and some dust tufts came away from his scalp.

"Hmm," Octavia said, looking on.

“Have *you* gotten any writing done?” Phil pressed to her, like they were besties. Octavia wanted to scream in his face and run, but Amander was there, watching, so she said, “I’m…thinking of maybe doing an erotic JFK Assassination…but I’m not sure which parts should be erotic. I keep thinking about doing stuff with the…bits that came out of JFK’s head, but…is that in poor taste?”

“Certainly,” Amander nodded, concrete, as Phil pulled back in his seat, blushing.

“Oh, I don’t know…” he trailed off, seemingly fading away somewhere.

“You’ve upset him,” Amander said, smirking at Octavia, and she took a bite of the complimentary Quiznos she’d selected. Biscotti tuna salad.

“Okay…I’m going to go sit down.”

Amander put her hand out to stop Octavia. Her hands were soft like a child’s, and slightly damp because she had a little bit of diabetes that she self-managed by just drinking Ensure for most of her meals and hoping for the best.

“Sit next to Yoshi. Give him company.”

Octavia looked at her. She’d been planning to sit next to Philly, but when she looked back into the bus she saw Philly was sitting with Octavian, who had taken a cab on his own to the station because he didn’t want to get up earlier and go to brunch, saying, “I don’t like women. *Old women*. I don’t wanna eat with y’all.”. Octavia knew it was just because her son was afraid of breasts and had a fear of being smothered by them. He always screamed anytime a large-chested older woman tried to hug and snuggle him. He screamed like a banshee, like a maniac; it was so embarrassing.

Octavian *did* like Philly, but Octavia didn't know why. Philly wasn't likable at all, an idiot, and her breasts were huge. *Weird kid,* she thought about her own son.

Octavia looked in back of Amander, two rows down, and saw a large-headed, moon-colored oriental fellow staring straight directly ahead of him, as if engrossed in some sort of performance. Maybe watching a play, or two white trash, big-boned crackheads fighting each other outside of KFC, asscracks on full display.

Yoshi, sensing Octavia's glare, turned his eye to her.

"Jamal," he said.

"And tell Niggarette," Amander was squeezing Octavia's arm fat like a mom gripping her child, her biggest mistake, in the aisle at the grocery store, "That I can hear her diseased ass mouth yippin' and yappin' about my man."

My man, God! Octavia wanted to vomit.

"Tell her to close her sore-filled mouth where my man is concerned, or any man that isn't the bum who gave her that monster she can't get off her back. Or the crabs out of her coochie."

Amander looked super petty, and at her shittiest, sincerely saying the word "coochie". She looked stupid, and she usually never did even though she willingly took loads from the likes of Phil, who was from Canada.

"Alright," Octavia nodded, "I'll let her know."

Amander kept holding onto Octavia's arm fat, gripping it with intention. "You tell Niggarette that the only reason she's even still breathing is because you have a little crush on her. I'm not going to get rid of my friend's little crush."

She looked steady at Octavia for a while, saying nothing, then spoke again, saying, "Do you still have your little crush?.."

Octavia wanted to say no, because she was shy and did not like to talk about her lesbian stuff to the dick eaters. She also wanted to say No because enough time had passed since Octavia had met Nic at Buffalo Wild Wings and initially fallen for her. Now Octavia knew Nic and she thought she was gross, spiritually, and kind of dumb, and sad. She was still attractive, and Octavia was still attracted to her, but the broad had HIV and her favorite show was *Blue Bloods*, sincerely. Like, it's not a bad show, but why is that your *favorite* show? Weird.

But Octavia couldn't deny having a crush on Nic, even if that was mostly the truth. To spare Nic, Octavia had to lean into the stereotype Amander had built up in her mind that Ock was thirsting over any woman who even looked in her direction, especially a Nic-type who was very lipsticky and wore high heels to the zoo.

She couldn't risk Amander thinking Nic no longer had a purpose, even though that was very much the case. Octavia wasn't totally confident but she was fearful Amander would do something if she thought there was no longer a rightful place for her in the crew. Octavia didn't want any blood on her hands. She was already a lesbian. That was her one thing, she couldn't risk taking on another thing.

Octavia forced a tight smile, a line, and nodded, saying, "Mm."

Not a total lie. She hadn't really said anything at all. She nodded, but that wasn't admissible in court, probably. Though she did wonder how it'd look when all was said and done and she was getting her final judgement. She was confident a little bit of a lie with a head nod wasn't enough to get sent to the underworld where her grandmother was probably being forced to snap peas with her titties out in Satan's kitchen, but you never know. No one does. Or, Octavia didn't. She didn't know the rules.

Depressed, she carried herself on back to where Yoshi was sitting and sank down into the seat next to him, causing a bunch of air to puff out from the bottom of it and Yoshi to clamp his eyes shut and go “Arggh!”. Something had flown up in the dust and gotten into his eye.

“You bitch!” he shouted.

Octavia watched him rubbing his eye, and she watched him so long she started to laugh. She tried to conceal it by clamping it down but it just turned into a bunch of snorting which was even louder than the laughing.

Octavia saw Phil pop up from his seat and turn his ugly self around to ask, “Yoshi, are you alright?”

Yoshi furiously waved his hand for Phil to leave him be. “Yes, I’m fine! Turn around!”

Phil stared for a bit while longer before doing as Yoshi requested and turning his ugly self around back in his seat.

Yoshi looked at Octavia. He had a large flat face like a gigantic pale pancake.

He closed his eyes and said haughtily, “Jamal, I do not like.”

Octavia started to ask him if he was speaking about Phil when Yoshi put his cold, thin hand down to hold Octavia’s gently, like a ghost. “Jamal,” he breathed a long sigh, “why would you do this?”

Octavia looked at him. “Are you speaking to me?”

“Who else?” he asked with disgust. “Why did you put this debris into my eye?”

"I didn't," Octavia laughed, and she wondered why the man was holding her hand. Was he dying? *Don't touch me,* she thought, and a terrible chill enveloped her. "It got in there from the wind."

"The wind?" he demanded. "We are enclosed inside a structure. What is this wind?"

Octavia looked at him. "The bus wind."

"The bus wind," he repeated like she was the biggest retard. Was there bus wind? Somehow the debris had gotten into his eye. So it was either bus wind or magic, or maybe they were the same thing.

"Does your eye hurt?" Octavia asked, and she wanted to laugh.

Yoshi looked at her and intentionally squinted, "Jamal, yes."

Octavia couldn't contain her laughter, and felt happy about indulging in it. Yoshi looked on steadily at her, waiting and watching. He wasn't a real person, just like Phil. It was how they got friends. To continue amusing herself, Octavia said, "I have a cream that could help."

"Jamal, a cream for my eye?"

"Yes," she laughed, and she reached into her bag to take out the jeans cream while Yoshi demanded to know what was so funny.

"Do you think it's funny for me to have debris in my eye, Jamal?"

Octavia shook her head, "No, not at all?"

"Why do you laugh?"

"You remind me of Mr. Kim, my karate teacher. He always had things in his eyes. Semen, and things like that."

Yoshi looked at her with interest. "You do karate? You're quite large."

"I took it when I was younger, when I was about twelve or thirteen."

"Oh," Yoshi breathed a sigh of relief, gripping his chest. This was when Octavia noticed he was wearing an airbrushed t-shirt of Nikki Parker lovingly caressing a homosexually disgusted ass Mr. Olgevee.

Hmm, Octavia thought.

"Here is the cream," she said at last, and presented it to him gently.

Octavia had texted Ray after stealing the cream, asking how to use it; there were no directions.

"You apply it to the jean," Ray texted, like it was common sense.

"And then what?"

"Is this a sext? I have my child's father over right now for spaghetti alfredo. I don't have time for that right now."

"Which child's father? You have like seventeen kids…"

"Nick Cannon."

Gross, Octavia thought. She wouldn't let Nick Cannon in her home, let alone her womb. But she didn't say that, she just sent Ray the eyeroll emoji so she would think Octavia was jealous.

"Ox, don't be jealous."

Octavia rolled her eyes at the message. Ray only got serious and acted like a real person when she thought someone was jealous of her. Why would Octavia be jealous of fucking Nick Cannon.

I gotta stop finding bitches to fuck at the aviary, she'd thought to herself, and had never felt more alone. It was her type. Dumb birds. She didn't want someone with sense. And they wouldn't want Octavia. She was an idiot writer and drove a damn bus! She couldn't get someone serious, someone with real goals and ambitions! She couldn't get someone who's been to the dentist within the last twenty years. Someone who knew about and understood interest rates. She could only get what she got. Octavia felt depressed now thinking about this as Yoshi looked over the tube and squirted a bit out onto his finger.

"Jamal," he said, to bring Octavia back to the present.

She looked at him, sunken with the realization that this was her life. *I'm on a bus to Florida to read to retards and vagabonds at a library where they probably mostly only have magazines and tattered Bibles.*

"Cream for my eye?" Yoshi said, and he moved to put his finger with the dollop of cream on it up to his eye, right at the ball.

Octavia sighed with depression, defeated. "No," she said in her tired voice, "it's for jeans."

She rubbed the leg of her GirlPlus MissBig-sized FUBU jeans to demonstrate. "You smear it on your jeans and it heals them."

Yoshi looked on, processing, then said, "And eyes? It heals the eye?"

Octavia thought about it. "Maybe. You put it on the jean and it heals the jean and it heals you, too."

“I don’t have a jean,” Yoshi said sadly. “I’ll put it on my eye and see if it works like that.”

And so he did, and for an hour afterwards he screamed non-stop at the top of his lungs, no breaks. It was even more cringe than Octavian’s screaming when he got hugged by that heavy deacon’s wife at church and Octavia was so fucking embrassed all those ugly church people were staring at her and whispering loudly about how Octavian probably be up at the house getting beat and molested.

No, he’s just a weird kid! He takes after his special needs father! Octavia wanted to scream at them, but that wouldn’t have helped her case. Anyway, only God could judge her, and he was very good at that, wasn’t he? Up there on his little perch, looking down at everyone, like he was so perfect.

You're a deadbeat dad and everyone knows it, Octavia wanted to say to him. *At least I take care of my damn kid!*

Yoshi’s non-stop caterwauling had prompted Phil to humph himself back to their aisle to reprimand Octavia for not being a good hostess to their guest.

“He doesn’t know many African-Americans,” Phil chastised, “Only me from the soup reviewer circuit. And I bring him aroun-”

“You are *Canadian.* So you’d be African-Canadian, or Canadian-American.”

“I bring him around my friends and family and this is what he is seeing and experiencing? Imagine what he will say when he goes back to his kind. His…I think, Monogolians, and tells them of what he experienced with the blacks of America?”

“Phil, who cares?” Octavia said under Yoshi’s screaming.

Phil pushed a finger to his chest, saying emphatically, “I care.”

Octavia jerked her head back in horror because some emphatic spit had gone from his crusty lip to her own non-crusty (can't have crusty lips as a fish eater!) one. She started to heave but stopped when Phil began to convulse in the aisle next to her seat.

"Hyung!" he went, and he gripped at his side and stomach in pain. "Hyung!" and down he went to the floor and he began to seize as if he'd been tasered.

Octavian considered that someone had done a voodoo doll up of Phil and was presently jerking it around wildly to fuck with him.

Octavia felt pleased with this thought. She couldn't handle him herself, but someone out there could and would. Someone who wasn't afraid of Amander, had no concept of her. Someone who was free to get rid of this bitch once and for all - no hesitation and no guilt. Someone with sense. Someone whom Octavia could never get a date with in a million years.

They had to pull the bus over in some dinky little town so Yoshi and Phil could be taken to the emergency room.

—

"Stay ready so you don't have to get ready!" Yolanda burbled from her wheelchair. Everyone looked at her.

They were sat in the waiting room of the hospital, looking stupid, waiting for Phil, and to a lesser extent the stranger man Yoshi, to get patched up and put back right again.

They had been waiting in dumb silence. Octavia herself had been thinking *Let's just leave them.*

Who cares?

Leave Phil and his Japanese man. Why were they sitting there? Who was this for?

Octavia looked across from her to Amander who seemed perfectly calm, not concerned.

There's no way she actually loves or gives a fuck about Phil, she thought. She has to be doing a bit or something.

"That's what I always say!" Yolanda was saying, looking them all in the dry, strained eye. "Stay ready so you don't have to *get* ready!"

Apropos to nothing, Leece began to speak: "One thing I notice," she slightly licked her lips which were dry, parched, and she looked at all of them tight, "One thing I notice is a lot of people-" and she was speaking loud now, pointed, "*A lot of people*, seem to be undiagnosed special needs or mentally handicap." She paused and looked at them all severely, then continued. “So instead of having a caretaker or guardian assigned to them, they’re just out *loose* in the world.” She nodded at herself, in agreement.

Octavian said, “Is this a dig at me?”

Leece smacked her lips and shut her eyes tight, then popped them open in irritated surprise. “I have no fucking idea who you even are.”

Octavia hit at the air before her, saying, “Leece, that’s my son, Octavian.”

Leece grimaced with disgust, shuddering. “I always forget you have a kid.” She shook her head in disapproval. “That shouldn’t be.”

Octavia looked away in shame, in agreement.

“Stay ready so you don’t have to get ready…” Yolanda repeated, this time sad, deflated, as if she were drifting away, being pulled in by the abyss.

Leece glared in her direction with rage as Mary kicked lightly at Yolanda’s colostomy bag hanging low off her chair.

“Your bag is full,” Mary informed her.

“You’ll have to change it,” Yolanda reminded her, shyly.

Mary turned up her face, “I’m not changing shit.”

Leece whipped her head in Octavia’s direction demanding, “Who the fuck are these??”

“It’s Mary and her caretaker Yolanda,” Octavia said, and she couldn’t remember even really meeting Mary, or what she’d said, or how Mary had arrived on the trip, though she did remember Yolanda’s sidebang and that Mary had potentially killed some old man by poisoning his soup when she used to work as a home health care aide. Octavia couldn’t imagine grey-skinned Mary working in any sort of home or medical care capacity. The job must not pay well and they have to hire just anyone from the streets or sewers, Octavia thought, and then she had the idea, when she returned home, to apply for a position. It had to be better than driving a bus. She wasn't going to change any diapers or feed anyone - that's disgusting. But she had the idea that she could gain access to these invalids' homes, much more so than her meals-on-wheels work allowed, and she could be inside their homes, eating their food and rummaging through their bureaus and things. Taking as she pleased. The job would allow her unlimited access to these people and their possessions. Maybe they'd have some money lying around. Some change she could take from some abandoned grandmother's dresser and use to play with at the arcade. Without Octavian. She didn't like taking him to the arcade because she didn't like spending time with him. She wanted to have fun and not be irritated by his presence. This trip was different because it was for work so she didn't have it in her head that it was supposed to be fun, so she didn't mind him tagging along for this, plus they were going to Florida. Maybe he'd get taken by an alligator into the swamp and she could kind of wipe her hands of him. She would never intentionally harm Octavian or intentionally abandon him, but she wouldn't be like, *ruined*, if an alligator came out and dragged him back to its little lair in the bayou or whatever the fuck they got going on down there. Maybe a sinkhole? Was that a thing or was it just in movies?

Mary sighed full of cringe, like a teen embarrassed of their parent doing a jig in front of everyone at the mall. "I have to bring her or they'll put me back in the asylum."

Leece was asking Octavia, "What are you just dropping by loony bins now for skange?", when Octavia received a ding on her phone.

A text from Ray.

Octavia read it and was annoyed. She said to Philly, sitting next to her, "Ray's going back to Dubai..."

Philly made a face like Oh, this bitch gettin' shitted on...

Octavia sighed with depression.

"Girl, get rid of her. You can get any chick. You have dreads and drive a bus. Anyone who wants a proper stud will want you, so why are you depressed about some thot who is like thirty-four and her oldest child is twenty? Come on now…"

"Who is this about?" Amander asked, scandalized, interested. "The PTA slut?"

Octavia nodded, embarrassed, but also secretly loving all the attention she was getting. She was the only lesbun amongst them and whenever her lesbianic escapades came up in conversation she was treated like a celebrity, like Luther Vandross. She felt guilty, but she really loved how interested and all in her business her friends became when the lesbian stuff came up. They were sooo…*basic*.

Mary, making it weird, asked Octavian, "Are you okay with your mother having sexual intercourse with women?"

Octavian looked at her, weirded out by a strange adult establishing inappropriate intimacy with him, and he said, "No. Who are you?"

"I'm Mary, little penis," she rejoined, a threat.

Octavian looked to his mom for rescue. She shrugged as an offering.

Yolanda said to Mary, lightly touching her, "I don't think you should be talking to a child.."

Mary looked at her with burned eyes, "Is that what the judge said?"

"Oh, lord…" Barb moaned, sick and tired.

Yolanda folded her hands into her lap and everyone looked at her full, brown colostomy bag bobbing loose and wild off the side of her chair. "No, that wasn't a direct ordinance...but I think it's implied."

"If it aint in writing, then it aint it," Mary chirped in response.

Yolanda had to nod, "I would tend to agree. However, stay ready so you don't have to get ready..."

"Mom, who are these people??" Octavian cried for help, of flabbergast.

"I..I met them in the bathroom," Octavia said to him, shy.

Octavian's eyes widened, *"What?"*

"Well," Octavia pointed at Mary, "I met her."

"Don't point *at* or *to* me," Mary warned.

Octavia said to her son, "The wheelchair one is her court-appointed caretaker, and cousin."

"What the fuck is a court appointed cousin?" Leece asked, not necessarily interested, but it was something to do, to say.

Octavia just sighed with annoyance in response, then Barb suggested they all take a break from waiting and head out to the hospital caf to get some coffee, maybe a bite to eat.

"Gross, hospital food," Leece gagged, and Barb reminded her, "You had a Quiznos Cheetos Cheeseburger on the bus and farted so much you had an accident on yourself, and it emptied you, so to replenish yourself you got a complimentary Quiznos Cranberry and Turkey Stuffing Lasagna Stromboli..."

"Mom, why are you all in my business and mouth watching me and shit? I don't like that. This is why I stopped talking to you for three months back when I was trying to audition for *American Idol*. If Clay and Ruben can be up there, why can't I?"

"They have talent," Barb reminded her.

"Oh, *wow...*" Leece said, getting tears in her eyes.

"Why do we have to fight?" Barb said, getting scared. Leece was the temper tantrum kid and Barb didn't like confrontation. She didn't survive Civil Rights and R. Kelly for her to be going back and forth with some chick who nearly blew her asshole out doing the brussels sprouts diet and she had to have Barb drive her up to the emergency room and get part of her colon pushed back in and her sphincter sewn back together. Barb wasn't about to go back and forth with this stupid girl, the second daughter.

"You literally just said I'm not talented and put me on blast for having two sandwiches on the bus???"

"...I just mean you aren't as talented as Clay and Ruben..."

"Who the fuck is Clay and Ruben?.." Octavia asked and Amander hit her, laughing.

Did I do a joke? Octavian asked, pleased Amander was touching her, and not to stop and tell her to be nice to Phil or acknowledge his Asian.

Philly was able to mediate the little scuffle between her mother and sister, and then they all got up to go to the hospital caf, mostly just because it was something to do.

Octavia herself was glad to be up and moving and not sitting pretending she gave a shit if Phil or the work friend survived. If Phil died things would be more to Octavia's liking, but she didn't want to be sitting there in the waiting room hoping eagerly for someone to get deceased. It felt in poor taste and she was sure not great for karma. Octavia was sure that idiot God was all up in her thoughts like Barb be all up in Leece's mouth, watching her, all in her business. He would know about her impure thoughts, wishing death on a person, and she'd get sent down to Heck to snap peas in Hell's Kitchen with her ugly, mean ass grandmother. So she needed to keep it cute, which was impossible. The best she could do was force neutral thoughts, which was just her trying to look at things from her surroundings and think about them over and over again to override the bad. Lamp, lamp, lamp. Colostomy bag, colostomy bag, colostomy bag, colo–

"Girl, I got IBS, I aint eatin' that shit," Leece was saying, dismissing what looked like an egg salad sandwich wrapped in plastic garbage bin lining that Nic was holding up to Leece's nose.

"You got IBS, or you fucked your stomach up incorrectly doing the brussels sprouts diet?" Nic asked, smirking.

Leece looked at her, "Girl, you have HIV.", and she waved her off, and the interaction was completed.

Octavia saw Philly push up to her sister and whisper loudly that Nic's stomach is fucked up too probably from AIDS and cum, and Leece made a laughing face, like she agreed, and Octavia, watching them, was jealous of their bond.

Octavia's older sister Watterstein never liked her. She was sixteen years older and had always viewed Octavia as a stain, at best, and from a different time. They had different dads, and Watterstein's dad was a respectable professional. A doctor who'd had their mom as his side chick. He had tried to make her get an abortion but wasn't the have-her-killed type, so upon their mother's refusal, Watterstein was born. He never visited her, but paid on her child support at least. Octavia's dad sold fake life insurance to vulnerable elderly people and retards. Her mom had bragged about him once, saying how clever and crafty he was. His name was Zepherus and he had a wooden leg, like a pirate. When Octavia got her arm ripped off, and had to get her wooden one, that was the first time she'd ever felt any connection to the man she saw only once or twice in her entire life.

Watterstein tried to act all high and mighty because her dad was a doctor but she never even met him. She stood outside his practice once and watched him surreptitiously from across the street, in a donut shop. Octavia never had to watch her dad from anywhere because he didn't have a job and his position couldn't be located. When he could be located, he was typically in prison, and it was maximum security so there was no way to get a peak at him from a distance, from a donut shop.

Octavia couldn't even fathom having a sister she actually liked. It was for the best, probably. At least she never had to share her snacks.

The hospital food was too grim. Mayonnaise pita pockets. Applesauce that's just apple and water and no sugar. Oatmeal and it's just oats and water in a bowl, loose. "Burgers" but the burger bit is some veggie shit and it's bunless. And salad in a bag with no dressing. Just a bag full of leafs and some carrot strings, no sauce, no seasoning, no croutons - nothing.

"Dressing causes heart attacks, diabetes," the cafeteria worker had offered when Octavia asked if they had any Thousand Island or Ranch or *something* she could put on what was basically just grass.

"*Ma'am*, you're wearing a hairnet," Leece had said to the woman, whose half her face was melted down as if she'd been standing too close to an open flame for like, a thousand hours.

Philly tapped her sister on the arm, to prevent her from continuing, and they all decided to just walk away and head out to the gas station they had seen coming in, up about a mile from the hospital. Octavian said they'd at least have old dehydrated hot dogs sitting under a roller.

“Who is this young man?” Barb had said, gesturing to Octavian's head when he said that thing about the gas station hot dogs.

“Ma, it's Ock's son, Octavian,” Philly reminded the senile ole bitty.

Barb flinched, concerned.

She scanned Octavia's quizzical form. “..How is that possible?”

“Barb,” Octavia sighed dramatically, “we already talked about this. You already asked me this shit.”

“Don't be sayin' curses and shit to my mom,” Leece warned.

Mary said, “Who brings their mom on a gal pal trip? Are you five?”

Leece was taken aback. “Girl, who even the fuck even are you??”

“Do you see me with my mother?” Mary said smugly, and then she looked around fakely, as if trying to find the woman. “No mother in sight. You know why? Because she's dead. *Long gone.*” And she smiled evilly, creamily, at both Leece and Barb.

In response, Barb tucked her arm up under Leece's and you could tell she'd use Leece as her human shield if and when the time came for that.

“But you have a caretaker,” Octavian reminded Mary, and then he pointed to Yolanda, saying, “Wheelchair.”

Mary bent down to yell in his face, “*You* have a caretaker!”

Octavia, attempting to be motherly, play her role, reached to clamp her hand over Octavian's chest, to pull him away from the banshee into her bosom, but she forgot about his gigantic breasts fear and cringed with contempt when he began screeching at the top of his lungs.

When some hospital workers rushed over, concerned, Octavia took this as an opportunity to get rid of him and told them he'd been molested and needed to be looked at. So then he was carted away, and she could now have all the expired gas station hot dogs to herself.

Whilst trudging through the general roadside flotsam and jetsam, on their way to their desired destination, a truck pulled up alongside their little on-foot fleet and honked its horn. Octavia thought it was because Yolanda's wheelchair had gotten stuck in the mud and they'd abandoned her a few yards back.

"They'll help her," Octavia said aloud to no one.

Only Mary needed to be concerned with Yolanda's safety and well being and she didn't seem too bent out of shape about having to leave her behind.

"It'll toughen her up," she'd said. "Grow her bones strong. Maybe she won't be a virgin anymore when we return."

Out of the truck leaned a heavy, negro man, with teeth so long and so yellow they glowed in the night.

He said, shouting from his window, and clearly to Leece, "What's wrong witcho wig, girl?!"

"I don't know!" she shouted up to him. "Why don't you ask your mother!"

“Phulicia…” Barb warned, putting a light, old hand onto her second favorite’s perfectly human, not-wooden arm.

“The fuck you just say to me?” the truck driver gasped, foaming at the corners of his mouth. “*Eye’ll* knock your fuckin’ teeth in! I’ll knock that raggedy ass wig right off yo’ raggedy ass head!”

Leece just cackled maniacally while everyone else began hustling forward in fear. It was nighttime and the man was clearly some sort of demonic presence or something like why were his teeth glowing and shards?

Only idiot Leece would taunt him. And it’s not like he was even in the wrong. Leece’s wig was fucking CRAZY. It was like…it was not to even be explained or comprehended. But the closest thing to compare it to would be a pile of dead crows? And she thought she was killin’ it, too. She looked like one of those unhinged people who babble to themselves on the bus. Leece wasn't *quite* at that level in her life yet, so why was she dressing the part? Maybe she was practicing, because it was almost definitely her future.

The truck driver man disappeared from the window, and then they could hear the door open and close hard from the short distance they’d tried to put between their little crew and his truck.

“Oh, *lord*,” Barb breathed.

“He’s gonna come over here and shoot us,” Amander’s son Franklin assessed, shivering. He was wearing a thin blazer and underneath a fishnet tank top. He thought himself some sort of fashionista but he looked exactly like his father, who was a creature, and he played violin in his school band. What even songs are they playing at the football games that require violin? He was a loser.

"Who is that speaking?" Barb said. She looked at Octavia, in disgust, "Is that another one of yours?"

"It's my son, Barb," Amander said, irritated. If it were up to Amander, Barb would've been put down long ago. What use did they have for a senior citizen in the crew? It's not like she could fight; she wasn't rich. Why was she there. Best she could offer was mashing up food for them with her extra-strong dentures. And why would anyone need that? Maybe Yolanda? But she wasn't in the crew. She'd never be in the crew.

Suddenly they could hear boots pumping hard on the ground, and it was coming towards them, so they all started running as a pack.

"Come here!" the man screeched with a pained voice and then they were all truly scared.

Octavia thought maybe to recall back what she'd learned in karate all those years ago. But all she could remember was during hot days when Mr. Kim would come to the dojo and take off his gi and underneath would be his tight little white tank top, yellow at the neck and armpits. She could see his nipples poking through and would feel sick with longing. His head had been so long and wide, like a mask. He was inhuman, almost; godly. Octavia wondered if she became a lesbian because the one man she truly desired was so unattainable. She wondered if her psyche was just like *fuck it, fish*. If she couldn't have Mr. Kim and his long fluffy ponytail and even longer, fluffier head, then she wouldn't have any man. She wondered what it would've been like to fuck him. Not as a kid, because that's weird and probably illegal, but as the woman she was now. Big and sloppy. Dry, unkempt dreads. She wondered how long it'd take Mr. Kim–the pasty, clammy version of him she remembered–to peel off her GirlPlus MissBig-sized FUBU jeans. Would she orgasm before he got them all the way off? She wondered if that would be embarrassing or if it'd be a turn on? Would he lick up her cream and say it was all going to be okay?

Octavia felt sick thinking about this. She thought she was over Mr. Kim. She thought she'd buried that.

"God," she said out loud, and she was so far away from the present that she didn't notice the truck driver man hacking away at Leece with some sort of tomahawk or hammer or something.

"Oh my god," Nic said, dumb, and Octavia looked at her and she was back conscious and screaming.

Anyone who wasn't getting hacked to death started running, wherever, didn't matter, as long as it was away from the truck man. All Octavia could hear was blood curdling screams and she didn't realize the screams had been coming from her own self until she'd collapsed from exhaustion in a patch of grass and it had gone quiet.

Octavia lay in the grass, alone, and listened. She could hear screams and shouting in the distance and she wondered who was being killed next. She'd wished it was Phil, but she knew he was safe and sound in the womb of the hospital being poked and prodded by people who were only trying to save his life because they were getting paid to, not because they truly desired for him to keep going on being alive. Octavia hoped Phil understood this.

After a while of laying in the grass, Octavia felt like she had to take a shit, and she wanted a hot dog.

She listened and there was no noise.

She peeled herself up from the grass and felt a heaviness in back of and on top of her. She felt her blood sugar was low, which she always felt it was if she had gone for longer than an hour without having consumed anything. She stood from the ground and looked into the night. In the far-off country where it seemed they had landed, there was nothing to see. So Octavia walked on, hoping she was moving in the direction where the gas station would be, where there'd be a bathroom, and hot dogs, and maybe strawberry milk, though she knew she shouldn't buy any. She was pretty sure she was lactose intolerant. Every time she had any dairy her stomach curled in upon itself and started rumbling and bumbling, acting real ghetto. Every time, like clockwork. If she took even a sip of yogurt she'd be right on that toilet in tears, in agony–at death's door–a moment later. But she wasn't about to keep being alive if she couldn't eat shredded cheese straight from the bag or chug non-stop gogurts, so, gut-churning explosive diarrhea every day it would have to be.

Octavia stopped her walking, after she felt like she'd been walking for a million hours even though it probably had been more like three minutes, and she remembered her jeans cream.

She pulled it out of the large, infant-sized pocket of her GirlPlus MissBig-sized FUBU jeans and examined it, thinking of smearing it on.

It'd disintegrated through Yoshi's eyes and into his bones, but that was because the cream was for jeans, not for Japanese eyeballs.

Octavia wondered if she put the cream on her jeans, would it heal them and seep through to her and heal her, too? She was tired and in pain and desperate, so thought, why not. At the very least, she'd have something to report back to Ray, after she returned home from her trip to Dubai, *if* she returned, smelling of doodoo.

Octavia squirted out a large hunk of the cream, and she thought of Mr. Kim.

A piercing metallic din sprang up from the bones of her head and she screamed inwardly. Fighting off the thoughts, and shaking her head violently to do so, she then moved to begin smearing the cream on the front thigh of her jeans.

Upon touching the jeans, the cream pilled and turned into a solid, gooey sort of lint, dotting her jeans like a million little maggots.

Octavia got triggered seeing all the little wormy balls and she winced and shut her eyes to it.

To get rid of it, unhaveithappen, Octavia whipped the tube of jeans cream hard into the distance, and heard it thump on the air.

“Ow, what the fuck!” the night returned to her.

“Who throwin’ shit?” it demanded.

Octavia froze, and stood still in the dark. If they couldn’t hear her, they couldn’t see her. She was invisible to the world.

“If it’s that baboon from the truck, I'm tellin!” the voice warned. “Cuz I saw you whack that chick wit’ an ax! I saw whatchu did!”

It was Mary, Octavia decided. Somewhere out there, far into the darkness.

Octavia considered calling to her, but changed her mind. She’d only known the woman from the bathroom, for five minutes, and what she did learn of her was that she’d been in prison for a decade for trying to kill an old man. If Mary would put drainer fluid in some old geezer’s soup, some invalid who can barely hold their head up, what would she do to Octavia? Mary had no allegiances to Octavia. At least the old man was paying her to come to his house and help him take doodoos. Octavia thought of Ray. Then she thought of Mr. Kim again. How if you had to use the bathroom at his studio you would have to shit or piss in front of the entire class. His dojo was very small. The bathroom was right off from the main room. Opened right out onto the mat, like a little closet. Mr. Kim wouldn’t let you close the door. He said he didn’t trust any of them. Octavia never knew what that meant, what he thought they might do in there, but she didn’t mind. She would always ask to use the bathroom every class so Mr. Kim could watch her poop or piss. And he would. He didn’t seem into it like she wanted him to be. He seemed full of contempt. Resentful, disgusted, annoyed. But he would not take his eyes from her. Sometimes he would talk. *"Only use two sheets of the toilet paper. Your scholarship does not cover toilet paper."* And he'd say this when he knew, could see and smell, that she'd done a shit. It was a wildly erotic time.

Octavia screamed to disappear these thoughts, and then shortly after she heard a heavy thumping towards her direction. Not fast like the truck driver man, but slow, leaden.

Mary was before her now, saying, "Oh, I thought that man was killing someone else."

She sounded disappointed.

Octavia was back to the present away from *those thoughts*. Glad, she said to Mary, almost excited, breathless, "Where is he?"

Mary looked irritated in the night. "Who?" she said, but she wasn't asking.

"The man," and now Octavia was whispering. "The one who hit Leece."

"Who is Leece," Mary said, and again, she did not really want to know. She wasn't asking. "And *hit?* He hacked the shit out of that chick. Many times. She is dead! Deceased!" and at the end there Mary was screaming hard from her neck, as if Octavia was slow or hard of hearing and couldn't comprehend the concept of being not alive. Only, Octavia understood very well, and craved it.

Octavia then thought about how she had never particularly cared for Leece. She was crass, abrasive, kind of ghetto, even though she had Barb for a mom who was mostly normal and quiet even though she was from the older gen who, if their daughters were getting molested, they would just turn away and act like it wasn't happening. Though, thankfully, Leece and Philly were never abused in their youth. Leece had said she was too chubby and smelled like fish so the molesters weren't interested, and Philly said their stepdad Linus was “too small” (Octavia had thought she was talking about this man’s penis but she meant his legs and arms), so they were spared and so Barb got to be a “good mom” and she seemed normal and she was quiet so why was Leece the way she was.

“It sucks that she’s dead,” was Octavia's attempt at grieving her departed kind of friend.

Mary consoled Octavia by saying, “She was gonna go eventually. Someway, somehow. Best she got it over with sooner, rather than later.” And in her eyes was blackness. Octavia could see, in the blackness, the helpless old man gurgling, half to death from his poisoned soup. Maybe Mary was only trying to help him along. The sooner you get to Hell and get accustomed to the way of life done there, all the excessive, punishing rules, the sooner you’ll be able to get a little routine going for yourself; make the best of things.

Mary scanned Octavia’s form and her eyes landed on the jeans. She looked back up into Octavia’s face.

“Did that man…ejaculate onto your person?”

Octavia stood for a moment, considering what was less or more embarrassing: Mary thinking some deranged truck driving lunatic had jerked himself in her vicinity and splashed his cum onto her clothes, or Mary knowing it was the flop jean cream; Mary knowing about jean cream’s existence, and that Octavia had stolen it, and thought it a win at the time.

“Mmm,” she said, and then snapped chipperly, “Yep!”

Mary groaned an *“Ohh”*, and Octavia knew instantly she’d made the wrong selection.

But she could not undo what had been done, and she could not bear to speak about the jeans cream. In her head, in that moment, she decided to block Ray and never communicate with or acknowledge her again. *I can't keep having sex with someone who lets Nick Cannon do loads in them.* That was her excuse, but there was something just cripplingly embarrassing about the whole jeans cream debacle to her. She felt like maybe she just didn't "get" it, and she didn't want to say to Ray and have this flopsy bimbo judging her for not being *in tune with the cream*. No, she could not bear the thought, let alone having to actually experience it in real time.

Blocked, she thought, and her head throbbed as if a little man lived inside there and was banging heavy on the walls of her skull, screaming out in anger, in despair.

"I need to eat," Octavia said tiredly to Mary, who instantly moved to scanning Octavia's form again, this time as more of a performance than as a utility, and she said,

"You don't need *any* food."

"I didn't get any complimentary Quiznos on the bus..."

Mary looked at her, "They were making the sandwiches in the bavfroom. I peaked in and saw them piling sandwiches on the rim of the toilet seat."

She said the sandwich she had had hairs on it.

"That could be from anywhere," Octavia said. "The food they use to make the sandwiches–I'm pretty sure they keep like the lunch meat in a dirty closet on the floor. Like, not in a refrigerator. Just a dry closet. I have a business associate who works there."

"'Business associate'," Mary mocked, doing air quotes.

"And why did you eat a sandwich if you saw it was on the toilet?"

Mary scrunched up her face. “I was hungry, *Einstein*.”

Who the fuck is Einstein? Octavia wondered, curious. *Does Mary think I'm a jew?* She wondered if it was because of her long wallet.

Octavia didn't know how, but eventually they reached the gas station. She couldn't believe it. The trek had seemed endless, though in reality, they had maybe walked twenty minutes before seeing the big GAS MART lights which caused Mary to scream and curse and she fell to the ground and weeped with exhaustion, thankful beyond words.

At this display, Octavia felt embarrassed at her own pain and grief and hunger and despair. She hadn't been hacked, she still had her long wallet, all her orifices were unplugged and clear of debris, and she'd only suffered, in the most minor of ways, for a minimal amount of time. She felt awkward and dumb, approaching the big GAS MART lights. Mary was sobbing on the ground as if they'd been trekking through the desert without water for days. It was embarrassing to see, and Octavia was embarrassed with herself for relating, and being in whole agreement.

Inside the GAS MART, right up by the door, was a pyramid of avocados. Octavia considered being healthy and buying one. Just for fun, just for once.

She looked at the sign, and was taken aback.

She flicked her long LesbianPlus wallet at the display, “These shits like eight dollars a ball.”

The man at the counter, who was Indian, and who could hear her, said, “Healing elixir.”

Mary, who had picked up an avo ball to examine, put it down when he said that, and they both moved from the display to further back in the store where he could not see them as clearly, could not speak to them.

“You buy or you leave!” he shouted to them as they stood before the fridge, considering beverages.

Mary said, “I know he don’t be talkin’ crazy like that back in Mumbai. Them monkeys would tear his ass apart.”

Octavia said she didn’t think Mary should be referring to Indian people as monkeys and Mary said she was talking about actual monkeys. “They live in symbiosis with baboons and shit over there. Monkey’ll come right in your little shack and sit down and eat at the table like it’s your uncle or some shit.”

“I think you're thinking of Jungle Book…” Octavia said.

“Now who’s racist?” was Mary’s intelligent retort.

Octavia selected an entire box of coconut balls and thirteen strawberry milks for her purchase. Mary got a bag of black licorice and an empanada that was on the warmer alongside the hot dogs and cheese-filled tater tots. She was planning to get some of the taters but when she asked Mowgli what kind of cheese they were filled with he said “drip cheese”, so she declined.

Upon returning to the hospital, they ran into Amander, who seemed perfectly normal and well-adjusted, despite the fact that their friend had just been viciously murdered right before their very eyes. However, Octavia held back from being too critical of Amander seemingly being fine and alright after witnessing horrific violence being committed against a semi-loved one. Octavia, after all, had happily purchased thirteen strawberry milks and the only thing on her mind was looking forward to going to the bathroom shortly to shit her entire guts out. She hadn’t thought about Leece once after getting it set in her mind that she wanted strawberry milk. She thought about how Amander had probably experienced something similar. Initially being shocked or weirded out or whatever by the murder, but then consoling herself quickly with the promise of short term pleasures. For Amander it was likely to be her eagerness to get back to the hospital to gaze upon her beastly husband convulsing upon his hospital bed in unendurable agony.

They all had to go on. The world couldn't stop just because Leece didn't know how to buy normal wigs from online like everyone else. She bought her wigs from a costume shop because of their heavy after-Halloween discounts. You could get all types of wigs for like a dollar the day after Halloween. They were all poorly made and looked like something from a Tyler Perry film, but what mattered most was the cost, and that it was nothing. If only Leece weren't so ghetto and cheap, Octavia thought. Oh well.

"Oh, by the way, Yoshi is dead," Amander said contentedly, as if she were saying to Octavia Happy Birthday, or Feliz Cumpleanos, Abuela, if she were speaking to Octavia's alter, who was a Dominican grandmother.

Amander mimed wiping her eyes, "Whatever gel he put on his face burned right through to his brain. Sad."

Octavia thought *Who is Yoshi*, then she remembered and said, "Oh", incurious.

Amander said Phil would have to stay on at the hospital to undergo more tests and observation, so she couldn't continue on with the trip.

Octavia sucked her teeth. "Bro, just leave him here. You can text him for updates from Florida."

"I'm not abandoning my husband to go to Florida of all places. I was just doing it for a laugh, and that was something I wanted to experience *with him*. We planned to enjoy ourselves quite a bit sitting and watching you do your reading. I was very curious to see how *that* would go, and so was Phil, but now that he's on bed rest and can't attend, well, I'm no longer interested."

Jesus, what a cunt, Octavia thought. *I've gotta get better friends. Friends I actually like, who actually like me.* But it was so hard. And she was so tired and obese.

Octavia just moved from her, and she thought about blocking Amander from her phone and her life, as well. This dizzy broad really seemed to love her ugly husband. Octavia thought it was only an acceptable aesthetic for Beyonce, and then, not even for her.

I'll wash my hands of her, Octavia thought of Amander as she sat on the handicap toilet in the hospital bathroom, shitting for her life. She moaned in agony and then all of a sudden felt as if she were transcending want and desire. Pain and agony. She was transcending mere human foibles and problems. Petty superficial little goals and plannings. She was above all of it as her diarrhea turned to mostly blood, and she had nothing left inside her to give.

After wiping her ass full of dark blood for a very long time in the hospital bathroom, she emerged, ready to reboard the bus and carry on with her journey.

She didn't need any of them, she didn't want them. Not even in a petty sense, she was just able to be on her own little cloud and float along and be fine.

Back on the bus there was only Mary and Niggarette. Octavia was surprised Nic was still alive. If anyone was going to end up murdered, she thought it'd be Nic out of everyone. Octavia was mildly impressed.

Octavia said to Mary, "Where's Yolanda?"

"Why?" Mary asked her with a wide, exaggerated mouth. She tilted her head to the side. "Do you want to rub your little meat pocket on her??"

"Meat pocket?" Octavia asked in disgust. "How would that even work? Does her pussy even work?"

Mary nodded to herself, saying, "I'm sure you would like to know."

"I wouldn't. I do not want to do anything with or to your cousin. She is in a wheelchair and uses an oxygen tank..."

Mary cocked her brow, curious. *"So you're too good for her?"*

"She would break or die or something if we tried to have sex."

Mary sucked her teeth, not buying it. Waving her off, she said, "You're just shy."

Walking further to the back of the bus, Octavia wondered if Mary was right. Was she too shy? Was she holding herself back from true love because of fear? Octavia didn't think Yolanda to be her type. Not because of her wheelchair, but because of her colostomy bag. It was bad enough to endure Ray's faraway tales of Dubai, but to have the shit bag right out front and center was a whole different arena. And Octavia doubted Yolanda was being paid to wheel around with basically what amounted to a fanny pack full of shid hanging off her waist. Octavia needed incentive to eat out a bitch with a pocketbook full of shit hitting her upside the head every time she goes in for a chew. It was too much. *Overly gay*. Octavia was only mildly a lesbian at best, she realized. She wasn't about to go to the dark side to get some pussy. She had her toe dipped cautiously, with disgust, in the world of Fish Guts. Shitty booty anything was not going to happen. She would never be that hard up; that horny.

Nic, late as hell, called to Octavia, saying, "Ock! Did you fucking *see that shit?*"

Octavia turned around in her seat and looked. At last, she said, *"Girl."*

Nic started laughing and clapping her hands, half from shock at what happened, and the other half because she was mentally delayed.

Octavia turned back in her seat with satisfaction. She had the idea to make an erotic novel about what had happened that night. Turn shit into gold. Or, shit into pennies. She only made like forty dollars a year in ebook royalties.

It took them until the next day but eventually they were in Florida. Octavia couldn't believe it really existed. She thought how it looked like anywhere else, except more disappearing.

Gross, I don't like it, she thought.

When the bus stopped at the Gator Gunk Bus Depot, as soon as she stepped off a hurricane started happening.

"What the fuck?" she said to herself as she was nearly whipped up into the sky to be returned to her maker.

Octavia turned right around and got right the fuck back on the bus.

"No, thanks," she said, shaking her head, and she sat back in her seat.

"Rest for thirty!" called the driver, and Octavia, now really looking at him, thought he looked like her grandmother, except with wider birthing hips. She watched the man clump off the bus, and felt depressed, and content.

She sank her head back on the chair and closed her eyes, then suddenly they snapped open and she thought with a panic, "Octavian!"

She took out her long phone to text him. *"Bestie?.."*

"wut?" he texted.

She breathed a sigh of relief. He wasn't dead. She didn't want him to be dead. Though she also was glad he wasn't with her, and didn't plan on spending too much time wracked with guilt over abandoning him at the hospital. He'd be fine. He was almost nine soon.

"Where are you?"

"Home!" wide-eyed emoji.

"You better not be eating my Fish Filets…" she typed.

Octavia always had a small stock of Filet-O-Fishes from McDonalds stashed in the bottom drawer of the fridge at home where the vegetables are supposed to go.

"Don't nobody want them nasty ass fish filets," he replied.

Octavia texted the rolling eye emoji. She thought about putting him on punishment when she got home, but that would require making speeches and shit and she didn't feel like talking to him. He was alive and everything was fine. And as long as he didn't touch her fish filets, there was nothing really to say.

Randomly, Octavia thought, *I should make an erotic novel about a homosexual karate teacher.*

She tried to snap the thought away. If she went there, she'd never come back.

I wonder if Mr. Kim is on Facebook.

"No!" she moaned to herself, shaking her head furiously, banishing the idea.

Octavia saw a bus person staring at her. *I look crazy.* She sank her head back on the seat again and tried to relax. She thought about Mr. Kim slowly pulling her karate culottes down when she first got her arm ripped off and was just starting to learn how to use the wooden one. She needed help using the toilet, or that's what she said to Mr. Kim.

He'd said "Ugh!" with disgust when she asked for help, then when her pants were down he exclaimed in horror about the state of her underwear.

"What are those?!" he'd cried.

They were shredded and tattered hand-me-downs from her grandmother.

Octavia moaned in agony at the memory. Her best memory. She quietly grieved over the crushing realization that she'd never be happy like that ever again.

She took out her last strawberry milk and took a large swig. The bus bathroom had since been quarantined-off with caution tape.

This was a suicide mission.

www.ingramcontent.com/pod-product-compliance
Ingram Content Group UK Ltd.
Pitfield, Milton Keynes, MK11 3LW, UK
UKHW021915190726
13853UKWH00002B/686

9 798798 681891